KaRaWa
and the
Southwind

Karawa

and the Southwind

George E. Koehler

Abingdon Press

Nashville

Library of Congress Cataloging-in-Publication Data

Koehler, George E.
  KaRawa and the southwind / George E. Koehler.
    p. cm.
  Summary: A fourteen-year-old boy whose father
was killed in an avalanche learns to overcome his fear
of the mountain glacier.
  ISBN 0-687-20700-2 (alk. paper)
  [1. Mountain life—Fiction.]   I. Title.
PZ7.K8177Kar 1988
[Fic]—dc 19   87-27339
                                                    CIP
                                                    AC

The quotation from Psalm 78 on page 5 is from the
Revised Standard Version of the Bible, copyrighted
1946, 1952, © 1971, 1973 by the Division of Christian
Education of the National Council of the Churches of
Christ in the U.S.A., and used by permission.

Manufactured in the United States of America

This is for Margie—
who loves the Wind.

I will open my mouth in a parable;
  I will utter dark sayings from of old,
things that we have heard and known . . .

Psalm 78:2-3a

CONTENTS

1. The First Step 9
2. Akori 20
3. Chosen by the Elders 31
4. The Decision 43
5. An Impostor 54
6. Blowing in the Wind 67
7. Winter Returns 83
8. At the Chasm 97
9. The New Story 109
10. Two Brown Acorns 117

1

THE FIRST STEP

KaRawa woke with a jolt. It was the great bell! Out in the yard someone was ringing the alarm—Four! . . . Five! . . . Six! . . . Seven! In a single leap KaRawa was at his window. He rubbed the frost off one of the panes and peered out into the night.

"The third time this week," he muttered. "Who could be lost up there on a night like this!"

He watched as the glow of candles appeared in other dormitory windows and the oil lamps in the yard below were lit. In the gleam of each lamp, a swarm of snowflakes danced wildly. Two bundled figures, then another, hurried to the left and out of sight.

KaRawa could feel the trembling begin in his legs.

Turning from the window he groped in the dark for his clothes. He was dressed in no time, but his fingers fumbled in the cold as he laced his boots. Then grabbing his sheepskin jacket, he bounded down the stairs and out into the circular yard of the village.

"How can they do it?" he asked out loud. Most people in NaKoma seemed to sleep right through the alarm. A few would go to their windows to watch a bit, then crawl back into bed. But not KaRawa. He wanted to be there as the rescue team made its preparations and left for the mountains. He just *had* to. Summer or winter, day or night, he had never missed a team's departure.

Slim and quick, he loped along the path cut through the snow, the falling flakes tickling his face. At the south edge of the village, he passed the last barn, big and black in the night, and soon the excited yelping of the trail dogs reached his ears. In another minute he could make out the amber light from the rescue hut not far ahead, and he broke into a run.

KaRawa joined several other observers in the wide doorway to the stone hut. His blue eyes gleamed in the lamplight. His hair, still matted and tousled from sleep, was long over his ears and fair as new-cut maple.

Inside the hut the eight rescuers were already fully dressed for the mountains—fur parkas, wool trousers, high leather boots. Some were adjusting their packs and adding ropes and ice-axes. Two were harnessing the dogs, while another was preparing a litter.

KaRawa was still shaking. Why did he always feel this way when the alarm rang? Something drove him here to watch—there was no way to avoid it. Yet his skin crawled with cold tingles and his knees were rattling like an old skeleton's. He knew that it wasn't the weather—he shivered like this even on warm days.

"Looks like an ice rescue."

KaRawa jumped. He hadn't even noticed the taller girl standing beside him. Her face was nearly buried in her parka hood, and he didn't recognize her voice. But as she turned toward him he could tell it was Lani. He had seen her a lot around the village, but didn't really know her.

"Ice rescue?" he asked. "How can you tell?"

"Their boots." With a mittened hand she pointed toward the team. "They're wearing ice boots. See the spikes?"

KaRawa nodded. He felt sort of foolish. He knew ice

boots well enough and could have figured that out for himself.

"Looks bad, doesn't it?" Lani continued. "Somebody must have wandered out on the Glacier."

The Glacier! A new chill shuddered through KaRawa's body. *The Glacier! Whoever it was must have been really lost to stumble out on that icy killer at night!*

In silence the two watched a young man light the trail lanterns. The rescue team was about to leave.

"You're KaRawa, aren't you?" the girl asked.

He nodded and tried to swallow the lump in his throat. He knew she was looking at him.

"I see you here every time I come. You must really want to be a mountain rescuer."

He turned toward her and smiled weakly. "Yes, I do . . . I really do. More than anything, I guess." But he dropped his gaze as he spoke. It was true. He *did* want to become a rescuer. But something was holding him back—something within, something cold and terrible.

The team was ready. With the other onlookers, KaRawa and Lani stepped to one side of the doorway as the rescuers and dogs left the hut's warm glow and pushed out into the night. There were four men, three women, and SaWilo, a boy not much older than KaRawa. As he passed, the boy's eyes met KaRawa's, but neither smiled. Both knew the risk of venturing onto the Glacier in the dark.

It was snowing harder now. In only seconds the lanterns of the team disappeared in the swirling flakes, and the onlookers turned to go.

"How about some hot cider?"

Lani's invitation surprised KaRawa, and he frowned. To be honest, he'd rather go back to bed, but that seemed like a dumb excuse. So as cheerfully as possible, he answered, "Sure, let's go." And stride for stride, the two set off for the dining hall.

The hall was one of the eight large buildings that formed the circle of the village NaKoma. Like the other buildings, the dining hall was built of huge logs, larger than a person could reach around. It was always open, day and night, and villagers often stopped by for a snack and conversation.

Inside, the walls were lined with flickering lamps and wooden plaques carved with the names of village elders and heroic rescuers of centuries past. The heavy round tables and chairs, hewn from oak, could seat the entire village of about three hundred persons. But at this hour there were only a dozen or so, huddled in small groups over hot drinks and relishing the fragrance of the new day's bread, already in the ovens.

KaRawa and Lani went to the kitchen. From a large pot on the stove, they ladled steaming cider into two brown ceramic mugs. Back in the hall, they found a table by the fire at the far end. Although the warmth from the red coals was welcome, KaRawa felt uncomfortable. Before tonight he had never said more than hello to Lani.

"Good cider," he murmured.

But Lani didn't answer. She seemed to be studying his face. "How old are you?" she asked.

"Uh . . . about fourteen, I guess."

"You guess? What do you mean? When's your birthday?"

"Well, I'm not really sure. They think I was nearly three when I was rescued and brought here. My father . . . you know . . . he didn't make it. And that was eleven years ago. So, thirteen or fourteen—somewhere in there."

"You were only three?" Lani seemed impressed. "Can you remember being rescued?"

"No, not really. Well, maybe a little. It's sort of vague."

"It must have been horrible!"

"Yes. I still have nightmares."

"So that explains your name?"

"KaRawa? Yes, 'the orphan.' I was never given a real name."

"And your father, did he have . . . ?" Lani was looking at his hair.

"Yellow hair? I don't know. I've never heard what he looked like." How often KaRawa had wished that he had the dark skin and brown hair of other villagers!

For a time they sipped their drinks in silence. Then Lani turned to him. "It's all right, you know. You don't *have* to become a rescuer yourself."

KaRawa twitched, then searched her freckled face, her large brown eyes.

"It's all right," she repeated. "The village needs people for all kinds of jobs. You could be a fire-tender or cook. I hear that we're going to need carpenters to build the new barns. You could become a carpenter. Or a weaver like me."

KaRawa was silent.

"Or a smith. How about a blacksmith?"

"I'm already apprenticed to Po the cobbler."

"Well, there you are then." Lani waved her hand in satisfaction. "Everyone needs shoes. As a shoemaker you will make a fine contribution to the village."

"I want to be a rescuer." KaRawa was watching the steam rise from his mug. He spoke slowly, deliberately. "I've always wanted to be one. I don't know why—I just have to do it."

"I think I can understand that." Lani leaned toward him. "But there's more, isn't there? What's the catch?"

Maybe it was Lani's voice, kind and reassuring. Maybe it was the cider with its tangy sweetness of last fall's apples, or the strange setting in the middle of the night. Somehow, for the first time KaRawa was able to confess his secret, to tell this girl what he hardly dared admit even to himself.

"I'm . . . " He swallowed.

"Yes?"

"I'm afraid."

In the fireplace a charred log rolled into the embers, releasing a shower of golden sparks. A small, new flame danced briefly, then went out. KaRawa continued.

"Have you ever felt there was something important for you to do, something just for you, something you were born for—and yet you couldn't do it? I mean, inside you couldn't bring yourself to do it. Or wouldn't. It was just too much, too big." He paused. "Too risky."

Lani was gazing into the coals. She smiled a faint, faraway smile, but did not reply.

"I *want* to," said KaRawa, "but I can't." He quickly lifted his mug for a deep drink of cider.

"KaRawa," began Lani.

Her use of his name seemed strangely formal. He wondered what was coming.

"KaRawa, I believe you can do it." She smiled at him and nodded confidently. KaRawa started to object, but she continued.

"You *will* do it. You *will* become a mountain rescuer, I know it. Why, you've already taken the first step—confessing your fear."

KaRawa looked at her doubtfully. "What do you mean? How does that help?"

"Oh, we all have our wolves, don't we?"

"Wolves? What on earth are you talking about?"

"You know, the enemies within us. My mother calls them wolves."

"You're not talking about real wolves?"

Lani laughed. "They're real enough! But they're inside us, not outside, if that's what you mean. I know I have one."

"So?"

"Well, I think the first step in taming our wolves is calling them by name—you know, speaking the terrible words out loud to someone else. By giving your wolf its proper name, Fear, you've already begun to rob it of its power over you."

"Do you really think that makes any difference?"

"Just wait and see." Lani grinned with assurance. "I think your wolf's days are numbered!"

"Hmmm . . ." KaRawa did not sound convinced.

For a while they talked on—about rescuing, shoe-making, weaving—but their eyelids grew heavy. Finally they returned to the kitchen to wash up the mugs, then headed back to their rooms for more sleep.

In the very center of the village stood the lodge, where all the people of NaKoma gathered every First Day, and other times as well. It was a round structure with walls formed of great granite blocks and with a roof of poles and thatch radiating from the center. It had four doorways—north, east, south, and west—and in winter each was covered with a heavy bearskin to keep out at least some of the cold. Just outside the west door stood a log tripod, from which there hung the huge bronze bell used to announce mealtimes, as well as village births, deaths, emergencies, and other events. Of all the buildings in the village, the lodge was the oldest. Some said it had been there a thousand years, and perhaps they were right.

It was the lodge of NaKoma—*NaKoma,* an ancient word that meant "the people who rescue." And that is just what this village was—a community devoted to saving travelers from danger and distress. Far and wide it was known as the Mountain Rescue Corps.

Everyone, from the youngest to the oldest, had a part to play in the special purpose of NaKoma. They were not all active rescuers, of course. But each had a role in the village's mission—to save those of other villages who happened to become stranded, lost, or injured in the rugged mountains and valleys above.

After breakfast KaRawa joined the stream of villagers making their way to the lodge, as they did whenever a rescue team was out. Inside, the curved hickory benches were arranged around an open fire in a circle about eight rows deep. KaRawa found a place on the front row, the innermost circle, while some of the younger children sat in the center on the floor by the fire. This Ever Flame, as it was called, was a small but cheery blaze, its smoke curling up to an opening in the center of the roof.

When everyone was seated, HaLona, one of the village elders, rose and went forward to stand by the fire. All grew quiet as she began to speak:

"Brothers and sisters of NaKoma, we all know that a rescue team went out last night on the very back of our old enemy, the Glacier. About midnight a fur trader from the Wolf River settlement stumbled into the village crying for help. He told us that just before dark he and a companion had foolishly tried to take a shortcut across the Glacier and his friend had fallen into a crevasse."

There were murmurs around the circle. HaLona continued.

"Our rescuers have been out almost eight hours now. As always, we gather around the Ever Flame to uphold them in their efforts. Any who wish to speak a word of support for these our friends and for the unfortunate trader may do so now."

For a time the only sound was the crackling of the fire. KaRawa was always uneasy with these times of silence, yet he had never quite had the nerve to speak up. Soon a teenaged girl rose and addressed the group.

Then an older man. And then Rok, another of the elders.

But KaRawa didn't hear a word. All he could think of was the phrase *fallen into a crevasse*. A crevasse! He had long since learned that to drop into one of these deep fissures meant almost certain death. And what of the rescuers themselves? How could they possibly return alive—especially with the new fallen snow hiding the dangerous spots?

Suddenly he remembered Lani's prediction: *KaRawa, you will do it!* A frigid wave of panic surged through his body. What if he were on that rescue team right now? He pictured himself dangling from a rope in a blue cavern of ice far below the Glacier's surface. Shuddering, he tried to wipe away the image.

No, he thought. *I won't do it. I can't!*

Dimly KaRawa heard HaLona invite everyone to stand and join in a closing song. The young lyre player, Lis, struck a few chords. It was one of those songs about the Southwind. Though it was familiar, KaRawa's heart was not in the singing. His voice was small, lost in the brave chorus around him.

> O Wind of the South, we praise you,
> Blowing through all of our days—
>   Winning us, warming us,
>   Freeing us, forming us,
> Wind of the South, . . .
>   We praise!
>
> O Wind of the South, we trust you,
> And follow you as we must—
>   Cheering us, chiding us,
>   Goading us, guiding us,
> Wind of the South, . . .
>   We trust!

O Wind of the South, we love you,
Gentle and swift as the dove—
  Touching us, tending us,
  Marking us, mending us,
Wind of the South, . . .
We love!

After the meeting ended, KaRawa squeezed between people crowding the aisle and found his way out the east doorway of the lodge. But he had taken only a few steps toward his dormitory when he heard a wild shout,

"They're back!"

With a whoop he turned and raced toward the rescue hut, stumbling through snowdrifts rather than taking the longer path around.

He stopped at the doorway, panting. The rescuers were already inside putting away their gear. Frantically he counted—two, four, six, eight—yes, they were all safe! But something was wrong. The rescuers spoke only a few words to one another, and in tired, low tones that KaRawa could barely hear.

Then he saw it. There in the snow by the doorway, still wrapped in gray canvas and roped to the litter, lay the frozen body of the lost fur trader. The team had been too late!

KaRawa felt the blood drain from his head, and he was afraid he was going to faint. The familiar shaking began again. Slowly he shuffled over to lean against the corner of the hut.

In a daze he watched the other trader and two of the elders arrive. He heard their muffled voices as they talked with the rescuers. He saw the elders embrace the downcast stranger. But it all seemed far away, as if in a dream. He laid his head against the rough granite of the hut and closed his eyes.

A mitten touched his arm, and even without looking he knew it was Lani. For a long time they stood there against the hut, not speaking. KaRawa was glad Lani was there. He remembered how awkward he had felt at first over the hot cider, but now it was good that someone who knew his weakness was near.

The body of the trader was taken away, and finally KaRawa turned to Lani and spoke.

"He's dead. He died out there in that crevasse."

"Mmmm."

"Don't you see?" he went on. "That could have been me . . . or you, or any of us."

Lani nodded solemnly. Then she spoke, not so much to KaRawa, it seemed, as to herself.

"Akori is not afraid of dying." She was looking down the long valley to the east. The snow had stopped, and far across the forested hills the plains could be seen, brown and hazy in the winter light. She continued.

"Akori says that if you trust the Southwind with your whole life, you don't have to fear anything. And it's true."

"What are you talking about?" KaRawa gave her a quizzical glance. "Who's Akori?"

"You know . . . the janitor. Akori, the caretaker. His workroom is over in the storage building."

"The old janitor?" he grumbled. "I don't get it. What does he have to do with my . . . my fear?"

Lani was still gazing down the valley.

"I'm not sure," she answered. "Something. Maybe a lot. You ought to get to know him sometime."

2

AKORI

At last—a sunny day!

It had been more than a week since the death of the fur trader, with nothing but dark skies and flying snow. KaRawa had ventured outside only to go to the dining hall and to his work with the cobbler. Most of the rest of the time he just stayed in his dormitory, playing games with others in the lounge or puttering in his room.

However, today was clear and warmer. And best of all, it was First Day—the first day of the week. KaRawa had been to the weekly village meeting and had eaten lunch. Now the afternoon was free, for First Day at NaKoma was a time of rest and recreation.

For a moment he stood in the doorway of his dorm, his eyes dazzled by the sunshine and snow. Beyond the lodge, beyond the huge log buildings on the other side of the yard, and high above the bare treetops, rose the peaks of the Back Range, shining in frigid splendor against the dark blue of the western sky. From left to right, as far as he could see, marched the mighty crags, led at the north by the mightiest of them all, the one they called the Bear.

KaRawa's eyes narrowed as he studied the mountains above. For a moment he clenched his fists, and his lips formed the word *yes*. Then turning to his right, he set off, coiled rope over his shoulder, an ax in his belt.

"Hey, where are we going?" came a familiar voice from behind him.

Oh no! he thought. *Just when I want to be alone!* He turned to watch Lani as she ran to catch up, her red wool jacket open and her one long braid bobbing from side to side.

"Isn't the sunshine great!" she cried, as she pulled to a halt. "What are you doing? You look like a mountaineer."

"Well, I guess I am." KaRawa grinned with embarrassment. "I'm going to try a little climbing. If I'm going to be a rescuer, I need to start practicing. I thought I'd climb the side of the quarry."

"Alone?" Lani's brow furrowed. "Isn't that kind of dangerous?"

For a moment KaRawa hesitated, then laughed. "Why don't you come along. You can pick up the pieces when I fall."

So with light spirits and bouncing step the two left the village and started up the North Track toward the old stone quarry. Soon they were deep in the hemlock grove, where only a little snow had managed to find its way through the heavy branches to the ground, and where now only an occasional shaft of sunlight fell. They looked in vain for the fresh green tips on the hemlock branches that would signal the coming of spring. Though the day was fair, winter would still have its way for a while.

They broke into a hardwood clearing, with the bare branches of oak, maple, and hickory above. Here the snow was deep but patchy, and they made a game of trying to find the easiest route. But before long they were choosing the deepest, most difficult piles of snow instead, until they both fell giggling into a shoulder-high drift.

After a rest they continued to the old quarry road and turned left. From there it was only a hundred paces or so up to the hollow where granite for the lodge and other buildings of the village had been cut so long ago. Entering, they stood on the flat quarry floor and looked up at the sheer gray walls.

Lani's eyes grew more serious. "Are you sure you know what you're doing?"

KaRawa studied the dark stone on all sides. Here and there were vertical cracks where an experienced mountaineer might find holds for climbing, but there seemed to be no easy route to the top.

"It's . . . it's not quite what I expected," he replied. "But I've got to make a start sometime—and this is it!"

"If you say so." Lani sounded respectful of his determination, but not convinced.

KaRawa chose an almost upright rock face with several narrow ledges that might support his climb. Not seeing any good way to use the rope and ax, he dropped them on the snowy ground. Then he threw his jacket to Lani and cried, "I'm off!"

"Be careful!" she called after him. And brushing the snow from a flat rock on the quarry floor, she sat down to watch.

In a few minutes KaRawa had made it up to the first ledge, about the height of two persons above the floor. There was some snow and ice on it, but it seemed safe. He looked for a fissure that might provide hand and toe holds, and saw one several paces to the left. Cautiously he edged along the shelf with his body plastered against the cold rock. Twice he almost slipped on the ice. The ledge grew narrower, to only the width of his boot, then less—and he soon realized he could not reach the crack.

"Dumb!" he muttered under his breath.

The only solution was to retreat along the ledge, but with his first step to the right he slipped again.

Desperately he tried for a new foothold, but it was too late.

"No!" he yelled. And before he knew it he was sliding down the rough stone face. With a "Yow!" he landed in some brush and loose rock at the bottom.

In a flash Lani was there, her eyes wide and wondering.

"I'm all right, I'm all right!" cried KaRawa. Wincing in pain, he managed to get up on his knees and, with Lani's help, to his feet. No, nothing seemed to be broken, but his right shirt sleeve was shredded and his arm stung like crazy.

"That was pretty stupid," he muttered with disgust.

"Are you sure you're all right?" With a worried look Lani was studying his eyes. For the first time, here in the sunlight, he noticed how many freckles she had. *There must be hundreds*, he thought.

"Let's see your arm," she said. He pulled back the torn sleeve and together they examined the palm of his hand and forearm, badly scraped and now starting to bleed.

"Ooo . . . it looks awful!" said Lani. "Let's get back to the village. That needs to be cleaned and bandaged."

"I suppose so." KaRawa's voice was low and glum. Lani helped him put his jacket over his shoulders, and she picked up his rope and ax.

Somehow the sunshine didn't seem as bright on the way back. Everything was spoiled for KaRawa. He'd failed as a climber, and worse yet, Lani had witnessed it. He'd probably be a failure as a rescuer too. Maybe he should stick to shoes and boots. *Even then I'd probably end up making a pair for two left feet!* he thought.

He slipped his left hand into his pants pocket and felt the polished surface of the shell, the cowrie he always kept with him. It had been found, they told him, clutched in his hand when they rescued him as a child. This small shell, brown and silver and white, was

KaRawa's only physical link with his unknown origins, and his fingers often caressed its surface in times of trouble.

KaRawa thought they would be heading for the little healing house, as it was called, out behind his dormitory. But once in the village, Lani bore right across the courtyard toward the southwest corner.

"Hey, where are we going?"

"To the caretaker's. Come on."

"Huh? The janitor's? I need a bandage, not a mopping."

"Akori has a way with wounds. He has medicines and bandages. He'll help it heal, believe me." By now they had reached the door to the caretaker's workroom. Lani turned and looked KaRawa in the eye.

"Besides, I want you to meet him."

KaRawa had often seen the caretaker around the village, walking with a slight limp as he went about his chores. But they had never spoken.

"I don't think this is a good time . . . " he protested. But Lani was already pulling open the heavy wooden door, and with a shrug he entered the room.

"Lani and KaRawa! It's good to see you. What brings you inside on such a lovely day?"

The voice came from an older man seated at a workbench, where he was repairing an oil lamp. His face was dark as leather and deeply lined, his hair and eyebrows thick and gray. Under a deerskin apron his chest and arms seemed as big as a bear's. But KaRawa was most struck by his voice—so deep and strong, yet so gentle.

"KaRawa has fallen in the quarry and needs a bandage," replied Lani.

Akori rose and stretched a hand toward KaRawa. "Well, let's have a look at it." Carefully he took the boy's right arm, lifted off what was left of his sleeve, and studied the wound.

"Hmmm. . . . Could be worse—*will* be better!" he smiled.

Lani gave KaRawa a reassuring wink as they followed the caretaker into another corner of his shop. There he opened an old wooden chest full of small bottles of all shapes and colors. Frowning, he chose one, opened it, and held it up to his nose.

"Ah, just the thing. This shouldn't even hurt."

As Akori cleaned and dressed the wound he hummed softly, a playful melody KaRawa had never heard before. The man's strong but careful manner, the tune, the rich odor of the workroom—wood smoke, cedar shavings, leather—all put KaRawa at ease. In fact, he found that he was glad to be here.

"Tell me, KaRawa. What were you doing in the quarry? I imagine this would be a nice day for climbing."

KaRawa gulped. He looked into Akori's gray eyes, shining under his bushy brows. He didn't want to talk about his stupid accident, but he couldn't lie in front of Lani. Besides, Akori seemed to know already. Why couldn't he keep these things to himself!

For another moment he hesitated. Then it seemed that there was no way to respond except to plunge in at the beginning.

"Well, somehow I've always wanted to be a rescuer. I can't say why, exactly. I like my job with the cobbler, but I feel that I am really meant to rescue people in the mountains. That saving lost people is my . . . my special thing to do. Know what I mean?"

"I certainly do!" Akori nodded. "I remember well."

Not quite understanding the caretaker, KaRawa continued. "I really want to do this. . . . I *have* to do it. But . . . well, there's a wolf."

"A wolf?"

"Yes, that's what Lani calls it. Something inside me that makes rescue work impossible."

"A wolf, you say. And does this beast have a name?" KaRawa swallowed. "Yes. It's . . . Fear."

"Mmmm."

"Sometimes I think I can overcome it. But then something happens—like the death of the fur trader— and I know I can never face the dangers of the mountains."

"I see," said Akori. "But where does the quarry come in?"

"Today I felt I could do it, that I could become a rescuer. Lani says I can do it."

"You *will* do it," interrupted Lani.

"Well, after lunch I just decided to get at it, to start learning to climb. It was dumb. I don't know the first thing about climbing. I guess I should stick to shoemaking."

"Hmmm. How's that feel?" Akori had finished the bandage and looked up at KaRawa.

"Much better. Thank you."

"You know, it's such a fine day. Why don't we step out back and sit on my bench in the sunshine?"

Sitting in the warmth between Akori and Lani, KaRawa relaxed. For a time they listened to the jays scolding in the treetops beyond the village. Finally Akori put his hand on KaRawa's knee, but he spoke to Lani.

"You know, KaRawa has good cause to be afraid of the mountains. I led the party that rescued him years ago. Oh, it was a dreadful night! Cold. Snowing. It must have been a terrifying experience for him."

KaRawa's mind went spinning! This old janitor had been a rescuer? A rescuer? And in the very team that had saved him? It was more than he could grasp.

"You . . . you were there?" he stammered.

"I was there." Akori turned to him. "Too late to

save your father, I'm afraid, but just in time for you."

"Then you saw my father?"

"Yes, son. And a fine man he must have been. He had covered you with his body to try to keep you warm."

Saved by his father! Then saved by Akori and the team! KaRawa realized he was lucky to be alive.

"Akori, tell me . . . did he have hair like mine?"

"Indeed! He was at least as fair as you. Now that has been a puzzling thing. In all our trade with other villages, in all our travels through the mountains and down to the lowland, we have never met people with light skin and yellow hair. Nobody can imagine where you came from."

Gloomily KaRawa jabbed at the snow with his boot heel. "No village. No parents. No name. All I have is my fear."

Akori glanced up at the jagged peaks beyond the trees. By now the sun had moved well into the southwest. Although the tops of the mountains were still edged in glistening white, the valleys were filled with the deep blue light of late afternoon.

"Come to think of it, KaRawa, fear is not such a bad thing. There's a lot up there to be afraid of. I've been afraid myself, many times."

KaRawa glanced up at him. "But were you afraid to become a rescuer in the first place?"

Akori smiled. "KaRawa, do you know the source of true courage?"

"I . . . I'm not sure I understand."

"You say that it's important for you to become a rescuer. That it's right. That you have to do it. Do you know where the courage comes from to be what you must be?"

"No . . . not really."

"Well, it has nothing to do with reckless acts of daring, such as your escapade just now in the quarry.

No, true courage comes from trusting yourself, trusting your whole life, to the power and care of the Southwind."

"The Southwind?"

Akori's words hardly made any sense to KaRawa. They were familiar, in a way. Many of the songs and stories shared at village meetings spoke of the Wind. But to him they had no meaning. He had decided that this kind of talk just went along with being part of the NaKoma family. Trust the Southwind? How could you trust a wind?

"Let me tell you a story." Akori rose slowly. For a time he stood surveying the snowy peaks above. Then turning to KaRawa and Lani, he sat on a convenient rock and began.

In the forest below Rocky Ridge there lives a certain stately maple tree named ToKala. Taller than the rest, she is known throughout the forest for her hospitality. Her branches give shelter to many a bird, and among her roots the chipmunks dig their winding burrows.

Like other maples, ToKala blooms early each spring, even before the leaves are out, and soon her winged seeds have matured and are released. Twirling merrily on the breeze, they descend slowly to earth, often landing quite far from their mother. And there some take root and grow.

Now one spring the seed at the very end of the very highest twig of ToKala's highest branch was slow to loosen its hold.

"I know I am destined to become a maple," it said. "Some day I will shelter the birds and chipmunks, just as my mother does now. But it is such a long way to the ground. If I let go, surely I will fall and be crushed."

The Southwind was wafting gently through the forest. As the highest seed felt the Wind's tug, it gripped its twig all the more tightly. The Wind gave an encouraging gust, sending other seeds flying. But the fearful seed clung to the tree, its thoughts on the hard ground below. Then ToKala spoke.

"Do not fear, my child. The Southwind is your friend. If you give yourself to it, it will set you spinning and carry you softly to some moist glade where you may grow."

The seed pondered its mother's words. They had the ring of truth about them. Yet there was the risk. It was such a long way to the ground.

The Wind rose again, and still the seed clung to its twig. ToKala spoke once more.

"Dear little seed, your life with me is past. Your future lies below in the nurturing earth. Trust the Wind. Only if you let the Southwind support you, can you become the maple you must be."

Still the seed hesitated. But a new thought was forming: It had come to trust its mother and her love. Then surely, the seed reasoned, could it not also now believe her words of promise about the Wind? Could it? Yes! Yes, it could. The Southwind too could be trusted. And on the very next gust, the seed cast itself onto the Wind.

Then what joy! Supported by the warm flow, it began its spinning—sailing up, not down—dancing over the hickory tops, then curling down among the bare white branches of the birch, up again and down . . . gently . . . gently . . . settling at last in the damp earth beside a large brown mushroom.

"It's true!" cried the seed. "The Southwind held me up! It held me all the way." And then, next to the mushroom, it began its work of becoming what it must be.

Again all was quiet except for the jays. This time KaRawa didn't mind the silence. It felt right. He wasn't quite sure what the story meant, but he liked it. He liked sitting here in the sun with his new friends.

"I've heard a lot about the Southwind," he said, turning toward Akori. "But I've never seen it."

"No one has seen the Wind," Akori chuckled. "But

tell me, KaRawa, you do feel its touch on your skin, don't you? You see it playing in the branches and skipping over the lake? You see the Wind at work, don't you, melting the snow, scattering the seeds, bringing the needed rain?"

KaRawa nodded.

"We cannot see the Southwind. But still it blows. In a strange way, past understanding, we sense its blowing in our lives. And we give ourselves in trust to its blowing."

The caretaker was looking intently into KaRawa's eyes. Though his face was old, it shone with the freshness of a baby's, and his gray eyes danced.

"KaRawa, this is the path to the courage you seek. Can you entrust your life to the Southwind?"

It was an appealing invitation. For a moment KaRawa caught a glimpse of a beckoning future, as if of another self in another world. Could he trust the Wind? Somehow it was not a question he could answer, at least not yet. He hardly understood the question, much less the answer.

As it happened, however, there was no opportunity to reply. The three were startled by the ringing of the great bell in the courtyard. Darting through Akori's workroom and out his front door, they saw people racing toward the lodge.

"What happened?" Lani cried. "What's going on?"

Stopping one nearly hysterical young man, the three heard the words that would change all their lives:

"Avalanche! Avalanche on the Bear. It got the rescue team. They're gone! They're all gone!"

3

CHOSEN BY THE ELDERS

KaRawa and Lani dashed for the lodge. There they found the people of NaKoma in an uproar. Some were shouting that there had been a terrible accident, but others denied it. Some thought the survivors were already back in the village, but others had heard that there were no survivors at all. And nobody seemed to know for sure who had been on the rescue team.

Finally old Ta, head of the village council, entered at the south door. Already bent with age, he seemed now to be carrying a heavy burden. The people hushed as he walked slowly to the center of the room. Then turning, he cleared his throat and spoke gravely.

"This is a dark day for NaKoma. I'm afraid the rumors you have heard are quite true. Yesterday a team of eight rescuers led by Ori left for an overnight exercise. They slept in the trail hut at the Great Western Pass, then went on to the Bear to practice snow rescues. Early this morning our scouts reported an avalanche in the area, and a second team was sent to investigate. Tragically, all members of the first party had been caught by the slide and swept . . . " Ta paused for an instant, "and swept into the Chasm."

31

There were sudden gasps—then only the crackling of the Ever Flame could be heard.

The Chasm! KaRawa had never seen the Chasm, and really knew very little about it. People rarely spoke of it, and even when they did, they quickly changed the subject. He had heard that the Chasm was a bottomless gash, black and hideous, impossible to cross—a gigantic abyss in which there was no life, no light, no sound, nothing at all. He knew that it cut from north to south just beyond the Back Range, thus forming the western boundary of their land. No one knew what country lay beyond—it was usually just called the Other Side. The thought of the rescuers falling into the Chasm—falling, falling, silently and forever—was more than he could stand. He heard a few villagers weeping softly.

Ta gave the names of those who had been lost. "Oh, no!" cried someone, and there were more muffled sobs. Several were men and women KaRawa had known, and one was SaWilo, the youth whose eyes had caught his just a week or so before as the team had left the hut in search of the fur trader. How could all these people be gone so suddenly?

Slowly, as if creeping up from his toes, KaRawa could feel his old fear of the mountains returning. Desperately he tried to turn his thoughts in another direction. But a picture of the avalanche took shape in his mind—thundering down on him, a wall of snow and ice and rocks—roaring, smothering, crushing, and then the black abyss!

"Who authorized this exercise?" An angry voice from the back shattered KaRawa's nightmare.

"Yes!" cried a young woman, jumping to her feet. "No one should have been anywhere near the Bear. With this warmer weather, an avalanche should have been expected!"

"Besides," shouted another, "that wilderness beyond the pass hasn't even been mapped!"

KaRawa glanced at Lani, next to him. Her tight lips showed that she too felt the tension in the air.

"The council gave permission," Ta answered evenly. "The team was on the west side of the mountain, untouched by the warmth of the morning sun. There was no reason to suspect any danger so early in the day."

But the hostile words continued, and KaRawa was quite amazed. Never before had he seen the people of NaKoma so upset, so divided. Some were accusing the elders of negligence in allowing the team to practice on the Bear, while others were trying to defend the council. Even the elders themselves seemed to be in conflict.

"Friends! Please, friends!" Ta finally succeeded in getting everyone's attention. "We cannot settle this matter here. I shall appoint a group of elders and others to study this accident and recommend how such tragedies can be avoided in the future. Let us now turn our attention to a more important matter, comforting and caring for the loved ones of those who have died."

There were murmurs of agreement. Again Ta gave the names of team members—"Ori . . . Kana . . . Wu . . . SaWilo . . ."—and the rest. Each was remembered with some brief words, and a special village meeting to celebrate their lives was scheduled.

KaRawa thought the meeting was just about finished, when several elders entered the lodge, and one strode up to the Ever Flame. It was Rok, the man responsible for training rescuers, short and sturdy, with a fringe of gray hair surrounding a large bald spot. He spoke firmly.

"The loss of eight rescuers in one blow is a personal tragedy for our whole family, but it also limits our ability to respond to any future emergencies, eh? There are only twelve other active rescuers in the village. Since we usually send out eight at a time, we can no longer meet two different needs at once. And there is danger that these twelve could be overworked to the point of exhaustion. Therefore, it is necessary to recruit immediately a new class of young people for training as rescuers."

KaRawa felt his throat tighten. *A new class of young people!*

"As you know," Rok continued, "no one in NaKoma is required to serve as a rescuer. In a sense we are all rescuers, for whatever our jobs here, we support the mission of our village, eh?"

KaRawa's tension eased a bit.

"But just now the elders have chosen seventeen young men and women to be invited for training, including some who are younger than we would normally select. Because of the emergency, the training program will be more intensive than usual. All trainees will be excused from their normal jobs. We'll work nine hours a day, six days a week, for the next fifteen weeks."

There were some whistles of surprise from around the circle. A rugged schedule indeed!

"I'm going to announce the names of those selected. If your name is called, please let me know by next First Day if you will enroll in the program. That gives you a week to consider this. We'll begin training the following day."

Seventeen to be invited. Hardly breathing, KaRawa counted as Rok named each person. He jumped when Lani's was the thirteenth name, and he turned to look at her. But she didn't move, and her dark eyes gazed steadily into the Ever Flame. He wondered what she was thinking.

Then "Holo"—the fourteenth name. "Ki"—fifteen. KaRawa began to breathe more easily. "PaWito"—sixteen. Then came Rok's final words:

"And KaRawa."

KaRawa couldn't remember what happened next. How did the meeting end? Where did he go afterward? He must have eaten supper. His mind was blank. All he could recall were those two words—*and KaRawa.*

Maybe he had imagined it. Maybe the final name had really been someone else's. No, there was no mistake. The sound was still ringing in his ears—*and KaRawa.*

He went to bed early, but couldn't sleep. Twice he rose to stare out of his window into the black, then flopped back into bed again. He had never felt so restless, so confused.

All night the awful choice lay before him. A mountain rescuer! What he had wanted and feared as long as he could remember was now within his grasp. In just fifteen weeks he could be a commissioned rescuer. He could be up in those mountains saving lives.

His thoughts reeled. At one moment he would imagine stretching out his hand to a forlorn child half buried in a snowdrift. But in the next he would feel himself twisting and tumbling, falling into one of the Glacier's deepest cracks. Or into the Chasm itself! Just when he was sure that he *must* become a rescuer, a frightful chill would shake his body and he would know that he could not.

It was toward morning of Second Day when he remembered Akori's words—that the courage to be what you must be comes from trusting your whole self to the Southwind. What did they mean? The words hardly made sense, but there was something engaging about them. Something warm and inviting.

It's worth a try, he thought. *Today I'll see about this Southwind.* And with that decided, he relaxed enough to fall asleep for a few hours.

He was awakened by the breakfast bell, but chose to skip the meal. Dressing quickly, he headed down the Cub Creek trail below the village. This time he was able to leave without Lani's seeing him.

The path dropped down into a ravine, and soon he was following Cub Creek, a small, noisy brook whose dark waters disappeared now and again under the ice and snow. It was a cold morning, but clear, and the icicles hung like white curtains on the steep sides of the little canyon.

After ten minutes or so he came to the three boulders where the stream angled off to the right, but here he turned up to the left. Squeezing between two of the boulders he entered a shallow glen of young maples, their smooth bare branches shining silver in the sun. This was his special place, his own private valley. He called it Fernvale, for in summer the hollow was carpeted from one side to the other with large green ferns. It was known, he was sure, only to himself.

KaRawa strode directly to a familiar stone, a chunk of granite about as wide as he was tall, level on top, with a maple tree at one side that made a convenient back rest. He brushed off the snow, sat down, and leaned back. Here in the quiet beauty of his secret retreat, the Southwind would surely find him.

Now and then bits of ice, warmed by the rising sun, tinkled and clattered through the branches to the ground. But there was no wind.

He watched for movement in the trees. He listened for a rustling sign. He turned his face this way and that. There was not the slightest breath, except his own.

He wondered if perhaps he was supposed to do or say something special. He tried to think of one of the village songs about the Southwind but couldn't remember the words. Growing impatient, he decided to try speaking to the Wind.

"O Southwind, this is me, KaRawa. You don't know me, but I live at NaKoma, the Mountain Rescue Corps. I've been asked to train for rescue work, but I'm . . . frightened. Akori says that you will give me courage. So please do it."

His words trailed off, strangely lost in the silence of the glen. He took a deep breath. The dry winter air was cold and refreshing in his lungs, but there was no breeze. He decided to try a more formal approach:

"O wonderful Wind of the South, come now into my life and fill my heart with the courage I lack."

Still nothing.

Perhaps he should be more firm. Standing on his rock and looking up through the maple branches, he tried to sound strong and important.

"Southwind! I call you to appear right now. Bring me the gift I seek!"

For several minutes KaRawa stood on his rock waiting, but there wasn't the slightest whisper of a breeze. And he certainly didn't feel any more courageous.

Puzzled and discouraged, he finally jumped down and trudged out of his Fernvale. At the boulders he paused and shook his head, then turned up the ravine toward the village. Suddenly he heard someone coming.

"I thought these looked like your bootprints, KaRawa."

It was Akori just rounding a corner on the trail and coming toward him. KaRawa frowned. Since he had been unsuccessful in meeting the Southwind, he'd really rather not talk about it, especially to Akori.

"How's that arm this morning?" Was it only yesterday that the caretaker had bandaged his scrapes? It seemed like a week!

"Oh, fine," answered KaRawa. "It doesn't hurt."

"Good!" Akori was before him now. Putting one large hand on the boy's shoulder, he spoke directly to him.

"KaRawa, I heard your name called yesterday. I know this must be a time of struggle for you. It's a tough decision, and only you can make it. If I can help in any way, just say so."

Hearing Akori's deep voice, looking into his eyes, feeling his touch—suddenly KaRawa no longer wanted to avoid him. From within came an urge to tell the caretaker everything.

"Yes," he said. "How about sitting down?"

The two whisked the snow off a log lying between the path and Cub Creek, and made themselves comfortable, with the singing brook before them.

"I . . . I didn't sleep much," began KaRawa, and he told of the long night's conflict. "So this morning I decided to come down here to . . . to a little place I know, and ask for the Southwind's help. Just as you said, Akori."

"Good. I'm glad you did."

"Well, nothing happened. I called for the Wind and waited for the Wind. I tried everything. Finally I just stood up and demanded that the Wind show up: 'Southwind!' I said, 'I call you to appear right now. Bring the gift I seek.' But even though . . . "

KaRawa broke off. Akori had jumped up and was staring down at him. His voice rumbled.

"You *what?*"

"I . . . well, I just cried out, 'Southwind! I call you to . . . ' "

"Do you presume to summon the Southwind? Do you claim to call up the Wind—'Blow now,' and 'Now stop blowing'?" Akori's eyes were blazing with an intensity KaRawa could not endure. Frightened and confused, he turned to watch the water falling over a rounded rock and disappearing under a shelf of ice.

"Boy, the Southwind is not at our command! Its ways are not our ways. It blows when it pleases . . . where it pleases. Yes, the Wind cares for us and our lives—even

more than we ourselves do. But it will care in its own
way! Do you understand that?"

KaRawa felt tears comes to his eyes. He swallowed and
continued to watch the water, *I don't understand anything*,
he thought, but he didn't want to say that to Akori.

"You said the Wind could give me courage. I thought
there was some sort of power . . . well, some magic it
could do. I didn't know what to say to get the power."

Akori's face softened. He kicked gently at a nearby
stone, then sat down again on the log. He sighed,
Smiling, he put his hand on KaRawa's arm.

"Excuse me, KaRawa, for being so cross. You didn't
know. Others who should know better make the same
mistake. They think the Wind is available to do their will.
I'm sorry, but it upsets me."

"That's all right," KaRawa mumbled.

"Let me put it this way," the caretaker went on.
"We've all heard stories about magic. Sometimes we
wish there were magic ways to solve our problems—that
if we were to rub a certain stone just right or repeat the
secret incantation, everything would be all right."

KaRawa nodded.

"But it's not like that in these mountains. There's
beauty here, and mystery and wonder. But there is no
magic. The Wind will not do tricks for us, no matter how
much we want it to. Nor is there any other magic force."

Slowly Akori's words took hold of KaRawa's mind.
There is no magic. No magic. In the moments that followed
he felt a whole world slipping away from him. It was the
world of make-believe, cherished since childhood—a
world of spells and counterspells, of strange powers and
fanciful creatures and transformations made in the
twinkling of an eye. Had he believed in magic? Not
really. Still, it had always seemed that if only he could say
the right words or do the right thing, the powers of
enchantment might grant his wish.

And wasn't the Wind such a power? KaRawa had begun to hope that the Southwind would give him courage—*zap!*—just like that. He could see now that it was not to be. The Wind was not a magician. Nor was there any other magic pathway to the courage he needed.

"Oh," he said solemnly. He felt even more desolate than before.

"KaRawa, I don't mean to discourage you. It's fine to ask the Southwind for help. It's important to do so. You have made a good start. But the Wind has many ways of working. It will answer in its own way, its own time."

KaRawa looked up doubtfully. Akori smiled and continued.

"You know, all this reminds me of the story of the three brothers of Mora. Have you heard it?"

KaRawa shook his head. "No. Will it help?"

"I think it will!"

The two settled themselves more comfortably on the log, and Akori began.

Not so long ago there was a small village named Mora, high on the slope of Mount Thunder. The dozen or so huts hung precariously at the edge of a deep gorge, so that during heavy snows and rains the village was always in peril.

One summer the worst happened. After several days of rain, a rock slide roared down from above destroying almost half the huts of Mora and injuring many residents. Worse yet, the slide ripped through the only trail to the valley below, completely isolating the villagers from the assistance they so badly needed.

It was urgent that someone reach the valley and bring back food and medicine. Three brothers went to the hut of the village chief and volunteered for the mission.

"It will be exceedingly difficult to find a way down the mountain," said the chief, "but be assured that the Southwind will blow, empowering you for the task."

On the first day the three men studied the mountainside

below, searching for a route to follow. It proved to be difficult, for Mount Thunder had been much changed by the rock slide. After long and wise consideration, they chose what appeared to be the best way to the valley.

"But," said the eldest at the end of day, "I didn't notice the Southwind blowing, did you?"

"No," said the others, "we've not felt the slightest breeze."

The second day was long and tiring. Sometimes with only a fingertip grip in the cracks between rocks, the brothers descended hundreds of feet down sheer cliffs. Many times they thought they could go no farther, but they shouted encouragement to one another and found new strength. By nightfall they reached the floor of a wooded canyon.

"We did it!" shouted the second brother. "But where was the Southwind promised by the chief?" For again the air had been still.

The third day the brothers started down the canyon, but soon their way was blocked by a river raging among jagged rocks. A narrow log stretched high across the churning water, but it seemed impossible to cross safely. Knowing they must try, however, they cheered one another on, and one by one they crossed on the log.

Finally, that evening they reached a village and told of the disaster above. A rescue party, with food and medicine, prepared for departure early the next morning.

As the men dropped into bed, the third brother murmured, "I wonder whatever happened to the Southwind."

The others wondered too, but they were too exhausted to reply.

After the brothers had led the rescue party back to Mora, the chief called the three to his hut and thanked them for their heroic efforts. They accepted the chief's gratitude and were about to leave, but it occurred to the eldest brother to speak.

"Sir, before we left you promised that the Southwind would blow, empowering us for this mission, yet we never noticed the Wind. All that we did we accomplished on our own."

Smiling, the chief answered: "While you were gone I

dreamed of the Wind. I saw the Wind blowing through your minds and guiding your choice of the best route to take. I saw the Wind blowing through every muscle and sinew of your bodies as you descended sheer cliffs of rock. I saw the Wind blowing through your hearts as you crossed a terrifying river. Tell me, was my dream true?"

For a time the three brothers stood silently before the chief, considering his words. Then they nodded, and the eldest spoke: "You dreamed the truth."

KaRawa watched as Akori closed his eyes and held his face up to the morning sun.

"I like the story," said KaRawa.

"Mmmm. I do too."

"Is it true?"

Akori chuckled. "My friend, we tell different kinds of stories in NaKoma. Some are about things that really happened. Others we create out of our life as a people—the inner voices, the stirrings, the dreams and hopes. But in every story lives the truth. For those who listen, each tale is true in its own way."

"And this one?"

"This story took place exactly as I have told it. It was nearly fifty years ago, when I was just a youngster. The story of the maple seed that I told you yesterday is a fable, a parable. But, KaRawa, do you see? They both are true."

KaRawa wasn't quite sure how a fable could be true, so he didn't reply directly.

"I only wish this Wind would blow in *my* mind, *my* body, *my* heart."

Akori rose from the log and looked down at KaRawa. Now it seemed that the caretaker's eyes were sparkling with anticipation.

"As I said, KaRawa, the Wind has many ways. I believe that in the days ahead the Southwind will be finding you."

4

THE DECISION

Late on the afternoon of Second Day, as soon as he was done at Po's cobbler shop, KaRawa started looking for Lani. Before long he spied her near the dining hall and raced over.

"We need to talk!" he blurted out.

"Well, you know me," she smiled, "a real chatter-bird."

"It's growing colder. How about here in the hall?"

"Sure!" said Lani, and the two entered through the double doors of heavy oak. As they wound their way among the tables toward the fireplace, KaRawa came right to the point.

"I suppose you're going to join the training program for rescuers."

"Yes," said Lani. "To tell the truth, I was surprised to be invited. I'm not really all that strong. But if the elders believe in me, I will do my best."

Her answer was so simple. Lani did not have the driving compulsion to become a rescuer that KaRawa did. Or the fear.

Pulling two chairs and a low bench up to the hearth, they propped their feet up before the fire.

"You mean that you can say yes just like that? How can it be so easy for you? Aren't you scared?"

Lani spoke quietly and evenly. "No, I'm not afraid."

"But I mean, of dying. Eight rescuers and a trader have been killed in just a few days. There were others last fall. There'll be more in the future—and one of them could be you."

Lani's eyes followed the lively flames. "I am not afraid of dying."

The words he could hear, but their meaning was beyond him. For KaRawa, death and fear were almost identical. How could anyone not be afraid, say, of the Chasm? He just shook his head in wonder.

"I know this doesn't quite make sense to you," Lani continued, "but do you remember what Akori said about the Southwind giving you courage?"

"Yes?"

"Well, it's true. I do trust the Southwind, KaRawa. I can't explain it, but I do. My life . . . well . . . it rests on the Wind. I'm ready to go wherever it blows. There is nothing I am afraid of, because I know the Wind supports me. Sure, bad things will happen. One day even death. But it's all right, because I'm surrounded by the Wind. That's just the way it is."

KaRawa watched her intently, listening to every word.

"Oh, it's nothing I've accomplished by myself." Lani crossed her feet on the bench. "I didn't squinch up my eyes and hold my breath and say, 'Now I'm going to trust the Southwind.' It's a gift. It's a gift of the Wind—and when it is given, all you have to do is accept it."

"Trust is a gift?"

"Certainly. It's a gift of the Wind in the family."

"The family?" KaRawa was lost again.

"*This* family, silly! The village. NaKoma. That's what it's all about. Here we live together and care for one another. And in caring we receive the gift."

KaRawa took his feet off the bench and leaned forward. With his chin on his fists, he stared into the fire, puzzling over Lani's words. Then Lani too sat up, and touched his arm.

"KaRawa, I didn't mean to call you 'silly.' "

"That's all right."

"No, it was wrong. No one is silly or stupid when it comes to trust. It's just easier for some people than others. I've lived in the village all my life. I was born here. I started learning to trust before I could talk. But others find the journey a long and difficult one. We're each different. My path has been easy, I guess. I can see that for you it's much harder."

KaRawa nodded solemnly. "Mmmm. I guess it is."

KaRawa and Lani talked on until supper and agreed to return to the fire, the next afternoon, Third Day. There was more talk then. On Third Night after supper, they stayed in the hall to play wali, a table game with small wooden cups and balls. Seated near the fire, they were joined by Holo, Ki, and PaWito, three boys who had also been invited to train as rescuers. The conversation turned to the decision they all faced.

"Are you going to train?" Ki asked the group.

"I don't know," PaWito answered. "I can't seem to decide. How about you?"

"Not me. Too dangerous. I have a good job in the kitchen. I'm going to keep on making soup!"

"What about you, Holo?" Lani asked.

"Yes, I'm going to do it." Holo leaned forward and spoke with clear resolve. "It's important. It's needed. And I know I can learn to be a good rescuer. Really, I can hardly wait till next week to get started."

KaRawa was glad Lani hadn't asked him. He still didn't know what his answer would be.

On Fourth Day, in late afternoon when the day's work was done, four of them met for a short hike—KaRawa, Lani, Holo, and PaWito. KaRawa and PaWito had still not decided about training. While the four walked they made up long lists of pros and cons, reasons for and against taking part in the program. As they returned to the village the reasons became sillier and sillier:

"Rescuers get to quit their other jobs when the alarm sounds!"

"They get to play with the trail dogs!"

"They get to stay up all night sometimes!"

"They get to travel to strange new places!"

And by the time they entered the dining hall they all were giggling.

The following night they met again by the fire in the hall for more wali and more talk. And still more the following night. KaRawa had never before shared matters of such importance with others—his fears, his life with no parents and no home village, his decision about training.

By bedtime on Sixth Night, as he made his way across the yard toward his dorm, he was beginning to feel that he really *belonged* to the village after all. He wasn't just the unknown orphan, but a real member of the NaKoma family.

On Seventh Day, the sun was shining brightly. The sky was a crisp winter blue, and in the tops of the trees the cardinals were singing, singing, singing.

"How about a picnic at Flat Top?" asked KaRawa after breakfast.

"Oh, let's!" cried Lani. Both had the day off, for the cobbler's and weaver's shops were closed on Seventh Day. They hurried to the kitchen to pack a lunch—some fresh buns, cheese, a small sausage, and two shiny red apples—and then they were off.

The trail to Flat Top zigzagged up through a snow-laden spruce grove above the village and out across the

Highland, as it was called—a vast rounded ridge open to the sky, and in summer covered with a vivid tapestry of soft grasses and small blooming plants. Here some of the snow had been blown away, and the recent sunshine had melted much of the rest. It seemed a good sign. Maybe spring was on the way.

KaRawa and Lani swerved off the trail and raced across the hillside, shouting and laughing in the morning sun.

"Look, I'm a deer!" cried KaRawa, leaping with great bounding strides.

"I'm an eagle! I'm an eagle!" shouted Lani, her arms outstretched, her braid and open jacket flying behind.

At the far end, the Highland dipped down to a creek, the last one to cross before Flat Top. Lani found some stepping stones and started over.

"One. Two. Three." But as she stepped on the fourth stone, it tipped, and her right foot plunged into the icy water well above her boot. Shrieking, she reached the other side—while KaRawa tumbled onto the dry grass in a fit of laughter, spilling the lunch in all directions. One of the apples rolled into the stream and bobbed out of sight over a small waterfall.

"That one's yours!" Lani shouted across the stream.

"It's yours, it's yours!" cried KaRawa.

Finally, breathless and still laughing, they were on Flat Top, an immense stone slab, nearly level and just right for picnics. As they ate they studied the plains far below, following the course of a broad river as it wound its way eastward into the distance. Some of the villagers had claimed to be able to make out the sea from here, a thin line of silver shimmering on the horizon. KaRawa thought maybe he could see it, but Lani wasn't so sure.

They shared the remaining apple and then lay back on the rock while Lani's sock and boot dried in the sun.

"I tried calling the Wind," KaRawa said suddenly.

"You what?"

"I told Akori about it. On Second Day I got up early and went to . . . to a place I know. I asked the Wind to give me courage."

"That's great!"

"Yes . . . but it didn't work. Nothing happened."

"What do you mean?"

"There was no breeze. There was no courage. It was just . . . "

"Nothing?"

"Nothing. There wasn't the slightest breath, except my own."

"What was that? What did you just say?"

"I said that there wasn't a breath of air, except my own."

"Your own breath?"

"Of course. I *was* breathing, you know!"

"Mmmm," Lani mused. "I wonder."

"You wonder what?"

"Well, Akori says that it takes a lot of wisdom to tell our own breath from that of the Southwind. He says the Wind breathes in us and through us, and it isn't always easy to know which is us and which is the Wind."

This was news to KaRawa! He sat up and looked down at Lani, his mouth agape.

"What *are* you saying—that my own breath was really the Southwind?"

"No, silly . . . "

"*Silly?*"

"Oops, sorry." Lani was sitting up now too, her arms around her knees. "But you know, the Wind is not going to knock you down like a gale every time. It may work very quietly . . . within . . . in your own breathing in and out. It may work among people who care about one another. It may . . . "

Lani stopped in mid-thought, for KaRawa was staring at her in wide-eyed amazement.

"Lani, tell me something! Do you believe the Southwind has been blowing in our lives these past few days—yours, mine, the others' by the fire? Do you think it has been offering me this gift you were talking about—the gift of trust—and I didn't even notice?"

Lani turned her face toward the horizon. A little smile played across her freckles, and was gone.

"I think you're right after all," she said. "You really *can* see the ocean from here."

That night KaRawa dropped into his bed, tired but happy. It had been a wonderful day in the sunshine, and so much fun to share it with Lani. *She's all right!* he thought. As he drifted off to sleep he was thinking again of her words the first time they met:

You will do it. You will become a mountain rescuer. And yes, he was beginning to believe her. Somewhere deep within him, beyond the ability of words to describe, he had begun to receive the gift. He had begun to lean on the power of some gentle blowing, soft and silent. And courage, like a tiny green shoot on the forest floor, was beginning to grow.

He slept soundly till just before dawn, when he had a terrifying nightmare. He dreamed he was leading a mountain rescue party along a narrow ridge that he had never seen before. He was excited about being the leader and felt proud and confident. Then suddenly it was snowing. Soon the flying flakes were so thick he could hardly see where he was going, and he knew a false step would send him and his team down one side of the ridge or the other.

He was relieved to see a figure ahead, which he thought at first was Akori. But as KaRawa drew near he saw it was a gigantic black wolf blocking his way. It

must have been nearly as tall as he was! The beast's
yellow eyes were gleaming, its snarling fangs were
bared. KaRawa tried to turn, but his legs wouldn't
budge—and the wolf crouched, ready to spring. With a
scream he woke up, shaking and sweating.

He could sleep no more. The picture of the
threatening beast simply would not leave his mind.
Even at breakfast he could see the yellow eyes, the
sharp fangs. He tried to tell himself that it was only a
dream, but the sense of helpless fright remained.

He was still troubled as he walked with others toward
the lodge for the weekly First Day meeting of the
village. As he took a seat beside Holo his mood shifted
from dread to panic. This was the day—the day he must
tell Rok whether he would train for rescue work. Last
night he had thought he could do it, but after the
nightmare he wasn't so sure.

The First Day meetings of the village family usually
had five parts. They began with a time for announce-
ments and personal sharing. Several persons had good
news to tell. Others shared their grief over the loss of
the rescue team members, or their sympathy for
surviving loved ones.

Next the songs. KaRawa had always enjoyed
singing. He liked the mellow sound of the lyre strings.
He liked the tunes, the rhythms, though he had never
paid much attention to the words. But today was
different. Several of the songs had something to do
with what he had been going through this last week.

For the final song the leader asked everyone to stand,
and for each verse, to choose a different person to sing
to. As the first verse began, KaRawa turned to a woman
sitting next to him, and they sang to each other:

> Wherever I look, whatever I see,
> I see the Wind,

The wandering Wind.
Wherever I look, I see the Wind,
Wandering now in me.

As he sang he remembered the different ways the wandering Wind had blown for the three brothers of Mora. He began to wonder if the Wind were not blowing in dozens of ways, hundreds of ways that he had never even suspected.

Feeling a tap from behind, he turned to face a smiling Akori, and they sang the second verse to each other.

Whenever we meet, whenever we touch,
I meet the Wind,
The beckoning Wind.
Whenever we touch, I meet the Wind,
Beckoning now to me.

KaRawa remembered Akori's touch when the custodian had first bandaged his arm, and later when they had met alongside the ravine. Was the Wind blowing then? Yes—now it seemed that it had been.

Lani was nearby, and the two turned to each other for the final verse. Her eyes were as wide and deep as he had ever seen them.

Whenever we speak, whatever we say,
I hear the Wind,
The whispering Wind.
Whenever we speak, I hear the Wind,
Whispering now to me.

Lani smiled broadly, but KaRawa was too absorbed to respond. All he could think was, *Yes! Yes! I have met the Southwind after all!* And in a pleasant daze, he sat down.

Then, as usual, one of the elders told a story, followed by a period of silence. KaRawa's mind went back to the words of the last song: wandering—beckoning—whispering. *Surely,* he thought, *surely the Wind of many ways has found a way with me! It has been blowing right here, here in the family, through these new friends of mine. . . . But can I trust it? Can I really trust my life to this Wind?*

The last part of every First Day meeting was a time for sharing decisions. Any member of the family who had recently come to some decision, big or small, was encouraged to stand before the group and tell about it. Then the villagers would promise to support the person in the new commitment.

KaRawa had never done this, of course, but now he knew the time had come. Along with two others, he rose and stood facing the family with his back to the fire. His knees were shaking and his mouth was dry. While the others spoke, he tried desperately to think of what he would say. All too soon it was his turn.

"I've been trying to decide . . . " His voice sounded hoarse and weak in the big lodge, and he could see that those in back were straining to hear. He started over.

"As you know, I've been named as one to receive training for mountain rescue work, if I choose. Well . . . others seem to find this invitation easy to accept, or to reject. But I don't. I've always wanted to be a rescuer, but . . . "

He choked and stopped. Suddenly, coming down the aisle toward him was a wolf, the great black wolf of his nightmare. It couldn't be—nobody else even looked at it. But yes! It was there—not ten paces away! Step by step it advanced, then paused and crouched—ready to spring—its white teeth shining.

KaRawa gasped for breath. In his terror he barely noticed that Lani had slipped from her place and was standing beside him, her sleeve touching his. He took a deep breath, and another. The wolf remained.

Then it happened. From some hidden reservoir

KaRawa drew a courage that he didn't know he possessed. It was a gift—a strange new sense that he could do what he must do. And standing taller, he looked directly into the creature's yellow eyes. For a long minute KaRawa held the wolf in his gaze, sensing his own power grow, and that of the beast fade. At last the animal hung its head, turned, and vanished into thin air.

For a moment longer all was still. Then, swallowing, KaRawa continued, his voice now strong and full:

"I could not have made this decision alone. But I've had some help." He glanced at Akori, who was smiling confidently, and then quickly at Lani beside him.

"Well, my decision is made." And catching the eye of the elder who had first announced his name, he gave his response: "Rok, I'm honored to be invited to train. I accept."

As the Corps rose to sing a closing song, Lani touched KaRawa's elbow and nodded toward the Ever Flame behind them. Turning, he saw that its slender golden tongues were bent slightly to one side, flickering in a soft breeze from the south.

5

AN IMPOSTOR

The rescue hut was a small stone building just above the village, alongside the trail most frequently used to reach the mountains. It had a sod roof, which in some seasons was fragrant with wildflowers, but now was covered with a thick blanket of snow. At the front was the wide doorway opening toward the trail, while at the far end was a fireplace, always ablaze in winter months. Short corridors connected the main room with the dog kennel on the right side and a storage room for equipment on the left.

Although KaRawa had stood at the doorway countless times to watch rescue teams prepare, he had never set foot inside. So as he entered the hut on this first morning of the training program, he was practically jumping with excitement. The room had its own distinctive smell—of dogs, boot oil, newly made rope, hickory smoke from the fire—and though clean, it had a worn look from centuries of use. Today it was alive with the tense chatter of the new trainees. KaRawa hung his parka on a wall peg and took a seat between Holo and PaWito in the semicircle of backless wooden benches near the fire.

Holo grinned. "Well, rescuer, it has begun!"

KaRawa just smiled and nodded. He was so pleased and nervous, he couldn't think of a thing to say.

Rok stood and the talk suddenly died.

"Welcome! In the name of NaKoma, the Mountain Rescue Corps—welcome! You have been selected to train for a magnificent work, that of guarding the lives of all who travel through these mountains, of saving the lost, the stranded, the injured. It is a hazardous mission you undertake, but an essential one, an honorable one. I'm glad you're here to prepare for this task. Our whole village appreciates your commitment."

Rok went on to explain that, of the seventeen persons invited, twelve had chosen to enroll in the program. He emphasized that rescue work was not for everyone— that probably, for one reason or another, not all twelve would finish the course and be commissioned as rescuers.

"That's all right," he said. "Though aiding travelers in the mountains is the chief business of our village, many different kinds of workers are needed if this is to happen. Let's see, KaRawa, you work for the cobbler, eh?"

KaRawa gulped. "Yes, sir."

"Well, by making shoes, and especially rescue boots, KaRawa has already helped to save lives. And so it is with the rest of you, whatever your job in the village may be. You all contribute to our primary task, whether or not you become active rescuers."

Rok then introduced the other three leaders who would help guide the training. First there was PaPaki, a tall, lithe woman approaching middle age, who had served in past years as a rescuer. She would direct the physical conditioning program. Briefly she outlined the daily routine of running and other exercises by which the trainees would build the strength and endurance needed. She said they would also talk about eating habits and other health practices.

In closing she laughed. "By the time I'm done with you, you'll be ready to wrestle a bear!"

Next was Ukima, a dark young man who was now an active rescuer. He would help the group with mountaineering skills. Trainees would explore and map the entire mountain range, each peak and valley, even the Glacier. In this way they would become familiar with every possible place a rescue might be required. They would practice climbing skills on snow, ice, and rock. They would learn to construct makeshift bridges and ladders. KaRawa's fascination grew, for this was just the sort of thing he was looking forward to.

Tiro, a jolly young woman from the healing house, would lead the group in rescue techniques—how to locate lost or stranded persons, how to treat injuries, how to transport persons who had been hurt. She would also direct their practice in handling and caring for the rescue dogs. KaRawa could see that Lani, across the way, had a special interest in this.

Finally, Rok said he would help the group understand more about NaKoma, the Mountain Rescue Corps itself—how the village first came to be, who some of its heroes and heroines had been over the years, what its mission in the mountains really was. Trainees would be telling and retelling the stories of the Corps and singing its songs. They would hunt for new meaning in the old words, and might even make up some stories and songs of their own.

As the group started off that morning toward Granite Gap on its first mapping expedition, KaRawa felt like doing cartwheels in the snow. Beaming at Lani he exclaimed, "This is it! We're on our way! We're going to be commissioned rescuers of NaKoma!"

"Don't get too cocky," Lani laughed. "Remember the stone quarry."

But KaRawa's enthusiasm was boundless. He

paused to throw a snowball at a tree trunk, then ran to catch up.

By the afternoon of Seventh Day, however—after six grueling days of studying, mapping, running, hiking, climbing—KaRawa could barely drag himself to supper. Every muscle and joint in his body was throbbing with pain, and his feet had blisters the size of river pebbles. And on First Day, the group's day of rest, he slept all afternoon.

The next week was no better. By Seventh Day he was as tired as he had been the first week. He had had no idea that the training would be so demanding. The leaders never let up, always asking for more, more. Two young men had already dropped out, but KaRawa was determined to keep going.

He had discovered why his name was the last of the original seventeen to be called by Rok. The names were given by age. He was the youngest trainee, and everyone knew it.

But, he told himself, *I'm going to be first. I'm going to be the best in the group.*

In some strange way, he was doing it for the Southwind. If he could prove that he was the finest rescuer of all, then surely the Southwind would blow in his life. The Wind would really know who he was and give him the courage he needed. So he tried to do everything just a little better than anyone else—to run farther, to climb higher, to make a better splint, a better map. No wonder he was tired!

The third week of training was entirely different from the first two. The group packed a week's supplies and, with a few of the dogs, set off for Elk Valley, nearly a day's journey to the north. There in a snowy clearing beside the river, trainees and leaders camped for the entire week. The schedule was more relaxed. They cooked and ate together, and had long hours for fishing in the winter streams, for visiting, playing, resting. Oh, PaPaki insisted that they continue to run and exercise twice daily.

But it was Rok who led most of their times together. He told NaKoma stories: The rescue on Flint Ridge. The long night at the Pinnacles. The old woman of Oka. The fire and the ice. Tapu and the five foxes. Rok also urged others to share the stories they knew.

On the second night out, KaRawa, in his zeal to be best, volunteered to tell Akori's tale of ToKala the maple and her seed. It wasn't easy to stand before the group, but he was determined. The next night he was more at ease when he told the one about the three brothers of Mora.

In fact, he found a new kind of excitement in sharing the old tales. By his words alone he could create new worlds. He could draw other people out of themselves and into the imaginative spell of a story, into its power and truth. Later in the week he was asked to repeat the tales of ToKala and Mora, and soon the group was calling him "the storyteller."

The last evening around the campfire, after Rok had described a particularly difficult rescue many years before, he asked the group a new question: "Why did you say yes to the elders' invitation? Why did you enroll in the training program, eh?"

"That's easy," Lis replied. "To learn to rescue people."

"But *why* rescue them? What is it to you?" With one hand the elder rubbed his bald spot as he pondered the question.

"Well," Simi offered, "we certainly wouldn't want people to die up in the mountains when they might be saved."

"But why you?" Rok was standing by the fire now, and his question was sterner, more insistent. "Why do you want to go up there and risk your necks for someone you don't even know? You think there's a lot of glory in rescue work, eh? You can name twenty or thirty heroic rescuers of the past, eh? Is that it—do you want to be heroes? Do you want your names up on the wall of the dining hall with the others? Do you want future generations to tell stories about your marvelous exploits?"

The group was very quiet. KaRawa struggled to think of a good answer to Rok's question, one that would impress him and the group. But he couldn't. In all his eagerness to become a rescuer, he had never stopped to ask *why*. It was just something he had to do. Rok might as well have asked why he wanted to eat, to breathe.

Rok went on, less harshly now. "I guess we all recognize that the question of why is not easily answered. Perhaps the answer is different for each of us, eh? But the question *must be answered*. Unless you are sure of your answer, you could falter at the crucial moment of some rescue operation."

"Why is that?" It was Kato's voice. KaRawa was glad she had asked for he didn't quite understand either.

Rok glanced around the circle. "You cannot yet imagine the difficulties and dangers of rescue work—rock slides, flash floods, treacherous ice, wolves, sometimes bandits, the sheer exhaustion of an all-night search! In almost any rescue effort there will be many reasons *not* to continue, many reasons to turn back. You must know in your heart a stronger reason—your very own reason—to press on and to succeed."

Rok paused. An owl hooted in the distance.

"At the final session of this training, before you can be commissioned, each of you will answer this question for me: Why do you intend to be a mountain rescuer?"

KaRawa felt a flurry of panic in his chest. He didn't have the slightest idea what his answer would be!

In the next weeks the same rhythm of training continued: two weeks of rigorous work, nine hours a day, six days a week—then a more leisurely week of camping at some remote site. By the ninth week KaRawa had come to look forward to these camp-outs. Two other trainees had dropped out, so now only eight remained. There were three women—Simi, Kato, and Lani; and five men—WaLoka, Lis, the lyre player, Holo, PaWito, and KaRawa. With the four leaders, they were like a little family within the larger village family, a corps of their own, with their own traditions, stories, songs, jokes.

As Storyteller, KaRawa had a special and honored role in the group. Rarely did an evening go by that somebody didn't ask, "KaRawa, tell us another. Tell the one about the rescue at Little Lake. About LapaPali and the bear."

Furthermore, in spite of his age, he had achieved a remarkable record as a trainee. On the skill tests given each week, he was now second in physical conditioning, third in mountaineering, and first in rescue techniques. When all the scores were combined, he was second only to Holo. How he wanted to be first! Surely then the Southwind would blow.

Holo was only a little older than KaRawa, but heavier and about three fingers taller. For some reason the two had never become close. When it came time for testing new skills, they were often rivals. KaRawa thought of everyone else in the group as a friend, but Holo he saw as the one he had to beat.

At the beginning of the tenth week, PaPaki announced another test in distance running.

"I've been warning you about this one. Earlier trainees have called it 'the killer.' Some of the terrain is rough, some of it steep. The whole course will take you about forty minutes. You'll run individually starting at three-minute intervals. As before, each runner will be timed with the water clock."

PaPaki described the course, which she had marked with strips of red cloth—down the Cub Creek trail to the Lowland road, then up toward the quarry, and back down to the village on the North Track.

"All right, runners. Are you ready? We'll start according to age, the oldest first. Simi, step up to the starting line."

As the runners left one by one, KaRawa's impatience grew. He was wearing his fastest shoes, a pair he had made especially for running. Though the day was cold, he had stripped to his lightest clothes. He was determined to win.

Finally Lani started. Then Holo. KaRawa thought if he could just beat Holo in this race he could take over first place in physical conditioning. Maybe Holo would slip on some ice or trip on a root. The seventh runner, PaWito, left the starting line. And at last it was KaRawa's turn.

He took off like a deer. But he had gone only a little way down the familiar ravine when a peculiar idea struck him. With the way the course was laid out, he could easily take a shortcut through Fernvale and reduce his time by maybe two minutes. No one knew about the glen, and no one was behind him to see him do it. That way he'd be sure to beat Holo.

Should he or shouldn't he? It wouldn't be fair, he knew. Rok would be disappointed if he ever found out. KaRawa thought he might even be dropped from training. Still, there was no way anybody could know. His feet pounded on the twisting trail, avoiding rocks and patches of snow where possible. Soon he saw the three boulders ahead on his left. What to do? He didn't have time to think. But he *had* to win! Here were the boulders—and almost unwillingly, he found himself turning up to his left and squeezing through the passage. He burst into the shallow glen he knew so well, across it, and up the other side.

A thicket of brush and rock slowed him down, and for a moment he thought his plan had failed. But then he saw the Lowland road ahead and broke through to join it just where a red cloth strip hung on a pine branch. Turning to his left, he dashed on. He could see PaWito ahead. Gradually he caught up, then passed the astonished boy.

On and on! He bore right at the fork and up the steep quarry road. Then a sharp left onto the North Track. He could see Lani ahead—and beyond her, Holo, who must have passed her. Now the village was in sight. And at last he lunged across the finish line just behind Lani. Those who had already caught their breath clapped and cheered, but KaRawa could only collapse on the ground, panting. His heart was thumping like a drum—and he knew it was not only from running.

When all eight runners were in, PaPaki announced the results.

"First place—KaRawa! Congratulations to our youngest and fastest runner! KaRawa, it looks like you won by at least a minute."

KaRawa tried to smile, but couldn't. He glanced at Holo, who was frowning at the ground.

"In fact, KaRawa, I think you have set a new record for this course. The water clock showed about thirty-seven minutes."

PaPaki went on and on about KaRawa's accomplishment, about how much he had improved during the training program. But KaRawa knew he hadn't really won, hadn't really set any record. The longer she talked, the lower his head hung.

Then Rok made a little speech congratulating KaRawa, and everyone applauded. It was awful! He had never felt so rotten. His stomach was churning with shame and fatigue. He stared at his shoes. For a moment he wondered if he should just stand up right then and confess what he had done, but that would be even worse. How stupid! He wanted to crawl into a hole.

That afternoon and evening were no better. And all the next day KaRawa's legs were heavy as oak, his face clouded and pale. It seemed that his friends in the training group had become strangers. They were talking and joking, but he didn't seem to be part of it. He was an impostor, that's what he was. They all might think he was a genuine trainee, but really he was a fake.

By suppertime he felt as if a great gulf had opened between him and the group. He was marooned on one side and they were all carrying on as usual on the other. Worse, they didn't seem to know that he was missing.

When he had finished eating he tried to slip out of the hall to return to his room, but he found Akori by his side. The caretaker put a large hand on the boy's shoulder, and after a few steps, he spoke:

"Well, KaRawa, it certainly has been a lovely Third Day. I believe there's the smell of spring in the air."

"Yes." KaRawa tried to sound as cheerful as possible.

"But you know," Akori continued, "sometimes it can be clear and sunny all around us but dreary within. True?"

KaRawa swallowed. "Yes, sir."

"Want to tell me about it?"

KaRawa looked up. For one wild moment he was afraid that Akori had found out about his cheating. Then suddenly it didn't matter. Akori was the one person who needed to know, who *had* to know, if KaRawa was to find his way out of this mess.

"Yes, I want to tell you."

"I'm listening."

On their way to Akori's workroom, KaRawa explained briefly how the training group had become such a close family and how well he was doing as a trainee.

"I really want to be first, to be the best in the group."

"Oh? May I ask why?"

"It's for the Wind, Akori. I want to please the Wind. I want the Wind to know who I am, to take notice, and really blow in my life. I think that's the way."

"You do?" Akori sounded skeptical.

They entered the workroom and pulled two chairs up to the caretaker's old iron stove. Its warmth felt so good in the gathering dusk.

"And are you first in the group?" Akori asked.

"Well . . . yes, I guess I am. Yesterday I won a race . . . only I didn't really win."

"You won, but you didn't win? Now that's a riddle!"

Although it wasn't easy, KaRawa lifted his head and looked directly into Akori's encouraging eyes.

"I cheated."

"Hmmm."

"I took a shortcut."

"I see."

"It was an individually timed race, so nobody saw me. They all think that I won . . . that I even set a record." KaRawa could feel the tears forming in his eyes.

"So then?"

"Ever since then it's been . . . the group seems so far away, and I . . . "

But by now KaRawa was sniffling and swallowing and blinking. The awful taste of guilt and unworthiness was more than he could bear. Akori put his arm around the boy's shoulder, and with a great flood of relief, the tears came. It seemed a long time before the sobbing stopped and Akori spoke.

"You know it was wrong, don't you?"

"Oh, yes. If only . . . "

"Tell me, KaRawa. Why was it wrong? What made it wrong?"

"Well, it was cheating. It was breaking the rules, plain and simple. And it wasn't fair to the others, especially Holo. If I had only . . . "

"Why else was it wrong? Why are you so upset?"

KaRawa thought a minute, but he couldn't come up with anything new. He looked expectantly at Akori.

"Well, I'm not sure, but it sounds like what hurts the most is that you broke the trust, the bridge of love and honor you and your friends had so carefully built. You destroyed the link with your family. And in doing so you cut yourself off from the care you need."

KaRawa pondered Akori's words. Yes, it was true. Even worse than being a cheat was being a traitor.

"What may be more serious, I suspect, is that you feel you have cut yourself off from the Southwind."

"Oh yes! The Wind . . . it will never blow now!" KaRawa hung his head. "And I was trying . . . "

"You said earlier that you were trying to please the Wind—trying to earn the Wind's favor by doing well as a trainee, by being first. Is that true?"

"Yes! I was trying as hard as I could."

"Hmmm."

It had grown dark in the workroom. Akori got up and reached for the tongs. Taking a glowing coal from the stove he lit two lamps, then returned the ember and added a log to the stove. KaRawa watched as the old janitor sat down and rubbed his hands in the stove's warmth. In the lamplight his gray eyes were glistening with an exquisite joy. KaRawa knew that something was coming.

"KaRawa, let me tell you of a Mystery—a Mystery

past understanding." He paused, then turned to the boy.

"There is nothing in the world you can do to earn the Wind's favor. The Wind is interested in *you*, not in your achievements. Whether you are first or last, strong or weak, right or wrong, it cares for you with the same full and endless love. When you are hurt, it heals. When you are lost, it guides. When you are afraid, it encourages. The Southwind cares, no matter what!"

For a moment KaRawa stood at the edge of the Mystery, sensing its depth, feeling its drawing power. Slowly he turned the words over in his mind: *The Wind cares for me, no matter what.* It was more than he could grasp. It was too big, too strange. Yet something deep within seemed to be saying yes . . . yes!

Akori continued. "You may think that by cheating you have put yourself beyond the Wind's care, that the Wind does not blow in those who break the rules."

KaRawa was watching the caretaker's lips, listening intently.

"What you did was wrong. In your shame you may want to hide from the Wind, so it may seem that the Wind is far off. But it is you who have run from the Wind, not the Wind from you."

"You mean it's all right with the Wind if I cheat?"

"No, it is not. But *you're* all right with the Wind, even when you cheat."

KaRawa shook his head. He was beginning to get lost. He needed time to think about all this. More than that, he needed an answer, a solution.

"Akori," he begged, "what should I do?"

Akori's eyes were still sparkling. He put his hand on KaRawa's knee, and with warm assurance replied, "You'll find a way, son. You and the Wind will find a way."

6

BLOWING IN THE WIND

Help! Help! Over here!" It was Lani's voice coming from a pile of jagged rocks at the base of the cliff.

"I'm coming!" KaRawa shouted back.

With his first-aid pack on his back, he scrambled awkwardly from rock to rock, finding her at last, sprawled between two boulders. The trainees were having a practice exercise in retrieving wounded people and Lani was playing a victim.

"Well, rescuer! Where have you been?" Lani's eyes were twinkling with mischief, but KaRawa did not respond. Instead he raised the question rescuers had been trained always to ask first:

"Can you hear me?"

"Of course I can hear you. I didn't fall on my ears, you know."

Then the second question: "Do you think you are injured?"

Lani responded as she had been instructed by Tiro. "Yes, it's here—my left wrist. The pain is unbearable. I think it's broken."

And the third question: "Is there anyone with you?"

With mock formality, Lani replied, "No, rescuer, not at the moment. You see, I was hiking to the Pinnacles with three chipmunks, but I fear they have continued without me."

KaRawa ignored her joking. By now he had his pack off and was digging out the supplies he would need—a couple of wooden slats, some wrappings, and a sling. As he started to fashion a splint for the injured wrist, Lani continued her lofty report.

"Actually, rescuer, one of the chipmunks tripped me. I cannot be certain, but I believe he did it intentionally. His name was Kuro."

But KaRawa was in no mood for fun. He had hardly slept all night. He had tried to put the cheating incident behind him, to pretend it had never happened. For a while that seemed to work. Then, like a cold shadow, the memory returned. And the words *cheat, fake, impostor, traitor* echoed through his head.

"Yes, it was Kuro. Have you ever met a mean little chipmunk named Kuro?" Lani babbled on.

Although he had tried, KaRawa hadn't been able to think of a way to set things right with the group, to feel like a full member again. He knew he didn't have the nerve to confess to everyone what he had done. Or even just to Rok. But this morning a new idea had come to him—what about Lani?

When Tiro announced after lunch that Lani would be his partner for the first-aid exercise, he started thinking about it—what he would say. All the way out to the rocks he had been practicing.

Now the splint was done, and he helped Lani to her feet. She sat on one of the boulders while he adjusted the sling to support her arm. The time had come.

"Lani, something happened on Second Day that I want to tell you about. It's . . . it's hard for me to say, but I need you to listen."

"All right. What is it?" Lani's deep brown eyes grew serious.

KaRawa began to describe his race experience. When he got to the point where he took off on his shortcut, Lani's mouth dropped open and she looked at him in a strange new way. KaRawa plunged on.

"Afterward I felt awful . . . terrible. Especially when PaPaki and Rok praised me so. I don't know why I did it. It was so dumb. Yesterday was horrible. Then last night I went to see . . . "

"How *could* you do that?" Lani had suddenly jumped up, her eyes wild and glaring, her fists clenched. "I don't understand! How could you *do* such a thing? How could you even *think* it?"

It was a Lani whom KaRawa had never seen before. She was beside herself with anger and amazement, and he could only stammer.

"Well . . . I didn't really mean. . . . The Wind . . . it was for the Wind . . . "

Now Lani was tearing at her bandaged arm. "After all we've shared together in the group! After the way the leaders have trusted us—and we've trusted each other! KaRawa, you don't deserve to be a rescuer. You're not even 'silly.' You're . . . you're a rat! a sneaky old rat!"

And with that she flung the slats, wrappings, and sling in KaRawa's face, turned on her heel, and disappeared over the rocks.

For a long time KaRawa just sat on the stone, mouth open and shoulders slumped. Lani had been his only thread of hope. With this tie broken, he was completely alone and adrift. Yesterday had been bad enough. Now he had nothing! Nothing.

Finally he rose and shuffled back toward the village. He decided to skip supper. Lani had probably told others by now about "the rat." How could he ever face anyone again? He went to his room and locked the door, a prisoner of his own making.

KaRawa was up at the first dim light of the spring dawn. From his window he watched the gray sky brighten over the black hulks of the other buildings across the yard. He was thinking about Akori's words: *You and the Wind will find a way.* Well, he had tried the only way he knew, and it hadn't worked. The Southwind? Did the Wind have a way he hadn't thought of?

Very quietly he dressed and left the dormitory. No one else was about as he headed for the ravine. He had resolved to go to Fernvale again. This time he would not try to command the Wind to come, but he would be ready whenever the Wind was.

Veering up between the boulders, he shivered. Here's where his troubles had begun. But as he entered the glen the chill left, and after going a few paces through the young maples, he stopped. Something was different. What was it?

By now the sun had risen. Its golden light was just touching the top branches of the trees, shining on the ripe, winged maple seeds and the tiny yellow-green leaflets. The air was still. The birds were still. KaRawa felt that the whole world was holding its breath, waiting for something new to happen.

He walked up to his stone and sat down, his back against the tree. Tipping back his head, he watched the sunshine descend through the trees, lighting one branch and then the next, and the next. He could hear his heart pounding in the stillness.

Then it began. High in the sunlight against the azure sky, the maple twigs started to bend, ever so slightly, then back. In another puff of the breeze they swayed again—and maybe a dozen glittering maple seeds began twirling their way downward.

KaRawa smiled.

Now a stronger gust bent the limbs, and suddenly there were hundreds, and still more—shower upon shower of golden seeds. KaRawa sat transfixed, following with his eyes one spinning seed after another—down, down, down—till it found its place on the ground.

Soon the breeze touched him. At first it was just a light caress on his left cheek—he wasn't even sure he'd felt it. But then it came again more strongly—and on both cheeks. Before he knew it, this refreshing breath of spring was surrounding him, streaming over his face and arms, bathing him in its fragrance and warmth. Now the seeds were falling by the thousands, shimmering in the morning light, twirling and gliding, up and down, all around him and all over him. What a morning!

The Southwind seemed to be holding him, filling him, loving him—yes, forgiving him. It was blowing not only *on* him, but *in* him and *through* him. And then he remembered Akori's words. Yes, this Wind was not interested in his scores. This Wind was not even interested in his cheating. It was just blowing—blowing in him here, now!

Then a new sound. He jumped off his rock and searched the glen, examining the treetops. It must be—yes, it was a song! Afterward he wasn't so sure he had really heard it. That is, he didn't know if it had come from the outside or from a place deep within himself. But it was a clear and certain song, a song of the Wind. Standing there with one hand on a young maple, and with the seeds still falling all around, he heard and remembered every word:

Whenever you come, wherever you go,
You are the one I know, I know—

O child of the Wind, the Wind, the Wind,
  You are the one I love.

Whatever you've been, whatever you've done,
You are the one, you are the one—
O child of the Wind, the Wind, the Wind,
  You are the one I love.

KaRawa had no idea of how long he stayed in Fernvale. Later he could remember walking up the ravine, humming the new song to himself.

At breakfast he looked around nervously, wondering if everyone now knew about the cheating incident. Lani seemed to have chosen a table as far as possible from him and would not look his way. But apparently she had kept the bad news to herself, for no one else seemed to be acting strangely toward him.

On the way to the rescue hut, KaRawa started talking with Kato. Somehow the experience at Fernvale had helped him. He was ready to rebuild the bridge between himself and the others. He didn't know how, but at least he now believed it could be done.

As was customary on Fourth Day, Ukima took charge of the training group to guide more practice in mountaineering.

"We've been learning the skills of rope climbing for several sessions. I think you're ready for a real test!"

There was a chorus of groans from the group, but it was in good fun. Actually the trainees were eager to put their new skills to use. Ukima began to pair the trainees for various exercises.

"Holo and KaRawa, I want you to try Pine Bluff—at this end, where it's steepest. It's tough, but you can do it. Should take about two hours."

KaRawa's heart jumped. He wasn't so sure about working with Holo. Would the older boy be resentful over his loss in the race?

"Well, let's go get it!" said KaRawa as cheerily as he could.

"Yes, what do we need?"

"Let's see . . . two ropes . . . canteen . . . "

"Lunch pack . . . first-aid kit . . . "

The boys selected the equipment required for the climb, then headed up the trail to the base of Pine Bluff. Once there, they carefully studied the cliff face, seeking the best route to the top. There was a tree here, a pinnacle of rock there, and various knobs, ledges, and cracks that could be used to support their climb. Finally they plotted a course in seven legs. The first three would take them to a pine tree on a broad ledge halfway up, the other four to another pine at the lip of the bluff.

"Who's leading?" asked KaRawa.

"How about taking turns? You could lead up to the ledge, then I could take the second half."

"Suits me!"

As they had learned from Ukima, the boys now examined the full length of both ropes for any signs of weakness. Their lives could depend on the ropes' reliability. Only one would be used on the way up. Holo carefully coiled the other for use coming down and looped it over his shoulder.

Finally they were ready. They tied the ends of the remaining rope around their waists, and KaRawa started up the granite wall, the rope trailing below him. Bending at the hips, he kept his body well out from the rock, so as to get the best traction with his feet. Jamming his fist or boot into a crack, grasping a spur with his hand, pushing up on a knob, testing each new support before trusting his weight to it, he seemed almost to flow up the cliff. At the first pinnacle he tied himself to the rock, looped the climbing rope around his body, then called down to Holo.

"Ready!"

"I'm coming!"

Holo did not use the rope for climbing, for its purpose was only to break a possible fall. As he advanced up the face of the bluff, KaRawa gradually pulled in the slack. Within ten minutes Holo too had made it to the pinnacle.

"One leg down—six to go!"

So they continued, up the next two legs toward the pine tree on the ledge. As KaRawa secured himself to the tree he shook his head in amazement. He could do it! He had the skill *and* the courage. How much he had learned in these ten weeks—about himself, about the mountains, about climbing!

"So far, so good!" gasped Holo as he clambered onto the ledge to join KaRawa.

"Halfway in less than an hour!"

"We may set another record today!" laughed Holo.

KaRawa's face clouded over. Holo's mention of a record reminded him of the wall still between them. He knew there had been no record set at the race on Second Day.

Holo led the final ascent, but it was not so easy as it looked. For much of the way, they had to rely on jamming fists and boots into vertical cracks in the rock. On the sixth leg KaRawa had a close call as a granite spur he thought was safe crumbled under his foot.

"Falling!" he yelled up to Holo.

"I have you!" came the reply.

And before he completely lost hold, he felt the rope tighten around his waist.

"All's well!" he called.

But his heart was pounding, and for a time he just

rested there. How glad he was for that rope! Then he
smiled. He knew his life was in Holo's hands, but he
had no fear. Roped together here, high above the valley
floor, he thought the two seemed more like brothers
than rivals.

On the last leg to the top, KaRawa suddenly
recognized what he must do to find his way back into
the training group. It would be the hardest possible
task—telling Holo himself about his cheating. After all,
it was Holo he had hurt the most by taking the shortcut.

At last KaRawa scrambled over the rim of the bluff to
join Holo on the pine needles under the tree that had
been their goal. There, as they sat resting, they had a
fine sunny view of the village, the wooded hills
beyond, and the now greener plains in the distance.
The village was just close enough to make out the tiny
people here and there, but too far to identify them with
certainty. They tried guessing who was who.

"That must be HaLona with the blue jacket," said
Holo.

"That one by the hall seems to be limping. It's
probably Akori," KaRawa guessed.

Finally KaRawa knew the moment had come. He
drew in a breath. The Southwind's song came to
mind—*You are the one I love.* He smiled to himself. And
still gazing at the village, he began.

"Holo . . . " His voice faltered. *Can I do it?* he
wondered.

"Yes?"

"Have you ever known the forgiveness of the
Southwind?"

"What do you mean?"

"This morning I had a strange experience . . .
strange and wonderful. I had done a really terrible

thing and was feeling awful. I knew it was wrong, but couldn't figure out any way to set it right."

"What was so terrible?"

"It was the race, the one down Cub Creek Trail the other day."

"What about it?"

"I didn't win."

"Sure you did. You had the best . . . "

"I didn't win," KaRawa repeated. "I cheated. I took a shortcut."

A flurry of barking wafted up from the valley. It sounded like a couple of the trail dogs were chasing squirrels. Then Holo spoke.

"I thought something was strange. Your time . . . it was almost too good to believe."

"Yes." KaRawa turned to him. "I'm sorry. It was dumb. I don't know why I did it. . . . Yes, I do. I thought the Southwind would take notice if I won, if I was first. I see now that it doesn't work that way."

"What doesn't?"

"The Wind. Akori says that the Wind cares for us whether or not we're best. Whether or not we're good. The Wind cares, loves, forgives . . . no matter what."

"Forgives?"

"Yes, that's what I was saying at first. I was feeling so rotten yesterday that I didn't know what to do, so this morning I went out to a quiet place and waited for the Wind. And, Holo, it came! It came and blew all over me, and in me. And it seemed I was forgiven. Forgiven! It was amazing!"

Holo stood up. He took a few paces to the right along the cliff edge, then back again.

"I don't understand," he said.

"I don't either. I didn't deserve it. I didn't even expect it. It just . . . happened." KaRawa was on his feet now too. "Holo, look at me." There under the pines high above the village the two boys faced each other.

"Holo, what I want to know, what I need to know, is this: Can *you* forgive me?"

Without expression Holo stared into KaRawa's eyes. Then he smiled.

"Yes. I think I know how you feel. It's all right. I forgive you."

"You do?"

"Sure. Let's just forget it."

"No, we can't forget it. I need to tell the whole group. I have to set things right again."

"Oh! Do you think you can do that?"

"I couldn't have yesterday, but now it's different. I think . . . I really do trust the Wind. And right now I feel that with the Wind's support I could face anything!"

KaRawa suggested that they break out the lunch. While they ate at the edge of the bluff they talked of how KaRawa could share his experience with the training group, and the two devised a plan. Late that afternoon in the hut, with Holo at his side, KaRawa was the storyteller again, with his very own story of doing wrong and feeling cut off, of his confession to Akori, of the Wind's forgiving love and the new friendship with Holo. As he spoke, KaRawa could see that at first some trainees frowned, some looked away or shook their heads. But by the time the whole story was told, they were nodding in appreciation.

Rok came forward and stood between the two boys, with an arm around each.

"We all know that what KaRawa did was wrong. In case you're wondering, we'll do the race again, so it will be fair to all. But KaRawa has also done several things right, eh?"

There were murmurs of agreement around the circle.

"He has recognized and confessed his own wrong-doing. He has accepted the forgiving love of the Wind. He has taken steps toward reunion with the one he injured, and now with this group, whose trust he violated. In these few days he has suffered a lot. I hope we can all help end this suffering by forgiving him and receiving him as part of our group again."

Rok then turned to KaRawa, clasped him by both shoulders, and smiled. "KaRawa, I for one, want to do just that."

KaRawa suddenly felt Rok's short, muscular arms around him in a great, squeezing hug—and in a rush the group joined in. He was surrounded by bodies and by a chorus of welcoming, forgiving words. It was amazing! He felt fresh and new—and best of all, reunited with his friends.

The clang of the supper bell interrupted the happy reunion. "Time to eat!" several shouted.

"Wait a minute!" It was Holo holding up a hand. "I think before we leave we should hear again the song KaRawa learned from the Wind and sing it together."

"Yes, yes!" others agreed.

So standing in a circle with hands joined, the trainees listened to the Southwind's song, then all joined in.

Whatever you've been, whatever you've done,
You are the one, you are the one—
O child of the Wind, the Wind, the Wind,
You are the one I love!

At supper KaRawa noticed that Lani was missing. This bothered him, but he was so busy with other friends that he didn't take time to think about it. Later, as he left the hall, he wondered if she felt as bad as he did about their last conversation and her angry outburst. How could they put that behind them and be friends again?

He turned toward her dormitory, not sure of what he would say, but determined to try to build a bridge. Taking the stairs two at a time, he knocked on her door.

"Who is it?" came a weak voice.

"Uh, Lani? It's KaRawa."

He heard bounding footsteps, and the door flew open. There stood Lani with red eyes and a blotchy face.

"Oh, KaRawa, you're here! You're here! Oh, thank you for coming," she sniffed. "Please come in."

KaRawa was glad that she wanted to see him, but he didn't quite know how to react to her tears. She had always been so strong, so confident. Her weakness confused him.

He stepped inside. "About yesterday . . . " he began.

"KaRawa, I was the silly one this time!" she interrupted. "A real beetle-brain. I feel so bad. Just when you needed me most, I wouldn't even listen."

"Well, what I did was terrible. I can see why you . . . "

"Terrible or not, there was no reason to cut you off. It was stupid and unkind—and I apologize."

KaRawa groped for words. "Yes, but . . . well, I really did cheat, you know. I think *I* would have been mad if someone else had cheated."

"I suppose so," Lani smiled. "But anger doesn't help, does it? What you needed was someone to listen, as Akori did, and Holo. Someone to forgive you and help you start over, as the Southwind did. I wish I had been able to do that." She looked directly into his eyes. "KaRawa, I'm sorry. It was . . . my private enemy. My wolf."

"Your wolf? You said once that you had a wolf, but you never told me what it was."

Lani smiled weakly. "How about some hot cider?"

"Sure! Then the wolf."

From a brown ceramic pitcher that had been sitting on the warm hearth Lani poured two mugs of steaming cider. As they sat down Lani sighed.

"If a girl always has the right answers . . . if she calls people 'silly' when they don't understand things her way . . . if she abandons her friends when they fail . . . "

"Oh, it's not as bad as all that!"

"It *is*, KaRawa. And worse. Around you my wolf has been practically asleep. But at other times, it can be a beast."

"Do you know its name?"

Lani's gaze fell to the brown bearskin on the floor at their feet. "Yes."

"And are you ready to name it out loud?"

"Yes."

For a moment the "beast" seemed to cling to its privacy, reluctant to be seen for what it was, even within the safety of this newly restored friendship. KaRawa waited. Finally—

"Pride." Lani swallowed. "Its name is Pride."

KaRawa was surprised. Lani never seemed to be vane about her appearance or boastful of her accomplishments.

"What do you mean, Pride?"

"Oh, you know how I always need to be good, to be perfect. I have to keep all the rules just so. I can't stand weakness in myself—or in others. It's a kind of arrogance, a pride of the heart."

"Mmmm." KaRawa could see some truth in Lani's confession. From that first night at the rescue hut, she had always seemed to be the very model of good

NaKoma behavior. She was the one who always knew and did what was right.

"I've always been a sort of know-it-all. More than anything it seems, I need to be right." She paused. "Oh, I can hardly bring myself to say this to you."

"Well, I'm glad you have. Maybe it'll be a first step in taming the wolf."

Lani finally turned to KaRawa and smiled. "I know it will. Thanks."

The talk turned to lighter subjects—the day's climbing, the possibilities for another picnic at Flat Top, and so on, until the cider was gone and the hour was late.

"I need to leave," said KaRawa.

But as they stood, instead of heading for the door, KaRawa turned to Lani. With his left hand he reached into his pocket and pulled out a small object.

"Lani, I was thinking today . . . well, if things worked out between us and . . . you know, . . . "

He could see that she was puzzled by his broken way of speaking.

"I was thinking I'd like to give you this. To sort of stand for everything being all right again. I'd really like you to have it."

Into her open hand he placed the shell. Its smooth oval back was spangled with brown and silver flecks, and the whole surface seemed polished to the highest gloss. As Lani turned it in her hand the white underside came to view, with its long, curved, serrated opening for the ocean creature that had once lived inside.

"Why, it's beautiful!" she said. "What on earth is it? I've never seen anything like it."

"It's a shell, a cowrie shell. It's from the sea."

"From the sea! How did you get it?"

"Oh . . . I've had it a long time." KaRawa evaded her question. Somehow he was not ready to tell her that the cowrie had come from his unknown past.

Lani turned the shell again to study its shiny back.

"The silver spots . . . they seem to form a pattern within the brown ones. A sort of . . . "

"A star?"

"Yes, a five-pointed star."

"That's what I've always thought."

"KaRawa, it's such a treasure! Are you sure you want to part with it?"

"Yes, I want it to be yours now. To show that we're friends."

For a moment more Lani hesitated, searching his eyes. Then she smiled.

"Well, thank you! I'll take good care of it."

In the dusk, as KaRawa crossed the yard to his dorm, he was bubbling with happiness. How good it was to be reunited with the training group, and especially with Lani! As he reached the doorway of his building he realized he had been humming again the song he had heard in the glen.

O child of the Wind, the Wind, the Wind . . .

7

WINTER RETURNS

The week had come for the trainees to make maps of the Glacier. Until now the only purpose of their mapping exercises had been to help them become familiar with the mountains. This would be different. The Glacier was always changing, and up-to-date maps were needed each year. The training group would provide the new, official maps for the whole village.

After lunch on Second Day, Ukima briefed the group on the mapping expedition.

"As you've probably heard, the Glacier is a slowly moving river of ice. As snow falls high in the mountains, it packs down, layer upon layer, and gradually condenses into solid ice. By its own weight this ice pushes slowly down the valley northwest of our village, destroying everything in its path."

"How fast is it coming?" Lis asked.

"Well, you can't really see it move by watching, but we have measured it with poles stuck in the surface. The ice seems to flow several hundred paces in a year."

"So it's getting closer and closer?" Kato sounded concerned.

"No, not really. It advances in the winter, but in the warmer summer weather it melts at the lower end. The toe—that's what we call the forward edge—the toe stays at almost the same place. Though the ice is moving downward, about the same amount melts away each year. Some years more, some less."

"How long is the Glacier?" asked WaLoka.

"That's exactly what we're going to find out!" replied Ukima with a smile. "And it's going to take all of us, trainees and instructors."

He then assigned pairs to different sections of the Glacier. One team would map the snowfield high in the mountains where the Glacier had its beginning. Another would survey the ice fall in the upper valley where the ice dropped steeply and was broken into irregular chunks. Others were assigned broad stretches of the lower Glacier and would locate major crevasses. KaRawa and Holo would map the toe.

"That may be the most important part," explained Ukima. "We need to know whether the Glacier has advanced down the valley since last spring or melted back."

"We can do it!" muttered KaRawa to Holo, nudging him with his elbow. Three months before he would have been scared to death to approach the Glacier, but now it was a challenge he relished. And just a week before he would have wanted to make his very own map, and make it better than anyone else's. Now he was looking forward to doing the job with Holo—and not so that the map would be best, but so it would help the village.

The group packed its tents and supplies and headed out on the North Track, then branched westward up the switchbacks of the Wolf River trail. By evening they had reached a clearing near the Glacier, where they set up a base camp for the coming two nights. The mapping itself would take all the next day, and they would return to the village on Fourth Day.

In the morning everyone rose early, and after a hot

porridge breakfast the teams took off for their assigned areas. For spring, it was unusually cold, well below freezing. As KaRawa and Holo strode along the trail, their breath froze on the fur of their parka hoods. And as they approached the Glacier, the air grew colder still.

Suddenly, as they rounded a rock outcrop, the toe came into view—an immense wall of gray ice looming above them and stretching to the left across the entire valley. The boys stopped. KaRawa felt a shiver go through his body.

"Whew! Look at that thing!" he exclaimed.

"Yes, look at it! It's gigantic."

"And so ugly. I thought it would be smooth and white."

"And powerful," added Holo. "Look at the size of those boulders it's carrying."

Stopped in their tracks by the awesome sight, the boys continued to examine the toe from one side to the other. This leading edge of the Glacier was dirty with all the rocks and rubble it had been carrying for years down the valley. Its face was carved into grotesque shapes by months of cracking, melting, freezing, cracking again. There were pinnacles here, caverns there, huge chunks of ice that had fallen free.

"Hush! What was that?"

KaRawa raised his hand, and they both listened. Again it came—a muffled creaking, then a groaning sort of thunder from somewhere deep within the wall. It was as if the Glacier were a living thing with a voice of its own, ancient and terrible. The giant was stirring.

"It's a monster," said Holo, "a deadly monster of ice. No wonder NaKoma people have always been afraid of it. Someday it will destroy everything, all the way to the sea."

"How could it?" KaRawa was skeptical. "It isn't going fast enough to get very far."

"I said *someday*. It may take hundreds of years, but sooner or later the Glacier will win."

KaRawa shook his head. He had heard people talk about the Glacier this way, but he wasn't so sure. Still, standing here with the great cliff of ice bearing down on him, it was easy to imagine the worst. There was certainly no way *he* could stop it—or the whole village, for that matter.

The two took from their packs the compasses, parchment, and other equipment they would need and began their day of mapping. Starting at the near corner of the ice, they worked their way to the left across its entire width. They took compass readings, paced off distances, and drew a careful new map of the shape of the toe and its relation to various landmarks of the valley—a mound here, a small peak there. It was not easy going, for the gravel surface below the toe had been deeply cut in past summers by the torrents of melting water from the Glacier. Fortunately, very little water was flowing on this frigid day, and they were able to cross the gullies without getting wet.

It was mid-afternoon when KaRawa and Holo reached the far end of the icy wall. There they took some time to rest and put the finishing touches on their work.

"That's one fantastic map!" exclaimed Holo.

"It certainly is!" KaRawa agreed. "I can hardly wait to get all the maps together to see what this thing looks like."

"Yes, then we'll know the whole monster, from head to toe."

They scrambled back across the rocks and found the trail to the base camp.

"Do you suppose they'll have supper ready?" KaRawa wondered.

Holo grinned. "They'd better. I'm starved."

But as they entered the clearing they were surprised to see that no supper was cooking. There was not even a fire. And two of the other trainees were taking down the tents and packing up.

"What's going on?" Holo yelled. "Where is everyone? Why are you packing, anyway?"

"We've got trouble," Simi answered, "big trouble."

"One of the teams had an accident on the Glacier," explained Kato. "I think the surface gave way under them. The others have gone to help."

"Who was it?" KaRawa demanded.

"They said it was Ukima and whoever was paired with him. Do you remember who that was?"

KaRawa remembered.

With a cold rush all the old fears surged up through his body, and the terrible trembling began again. Sinking onto a stone and hugging his parka tightly around him, he replied:

"Yes." His voice was flat and dull, and he stared blankly at the ground. "It was Lani."

For a moment nobody said a word. Then Simi explained, "We were told to pack up. They think there's an injury. We're all returning to the village tonight so that whoever is hurt can get to the healing house."

The others returned at dusk. KaRawa jumped up and searched the faces of the first arrivals. There were no smiles, no greetings. Then he saw Rok and Ukima, carrying between them a litter. Still shivering, KaRawa ran to meet them. Was it . . . ? Yes, it was Lani, her eyes closed, her face cold and pale and still.

"Is she . . . ?"

"She's badly hurt," Tiro replied. "She's not bleeding, but she's unconscious. We need to carry her very gently. And we need to get back to the village as soon as we can."

The supplies were all packed and Rok gave the order to leave. When the lanterns were lit the sober group started down the trail toward NaKoma. The temperature was still dropping, and soon it started to snow, making the trail dangerously slick. They paused to rope Lani to the litter so that there would be no chance of her falling off, should someone slip.

At one resting place KaRawa asked to take a turn carrying the litter, and PaPaki joined him. As he trudged along he looked down at Lani's face in dazed disbelief. The swinging lanterns were making huge jumping shadows on her, on everyone, on the snowy trees around them. It seemed like some weird other world.

With every step the same anxious refrain sounded through KaRawa's mind: *Oh, Lani, don't die! Don't die! Don't die!*

It was past midnight when they reached the village. While most continued to the rescue hut, KaRawa stopped with the litter at the healing house. Miwa, the doctor, was roused, along with his assistant, and they took Lani to the examining room.

KaRawa looked up at Tiro.

"What's going to happen now?"

Tiro put her hand on his shoulder and smiled. "She'll be taken care of, KaRawa. Don't worry. The best thing for us now is to get some sleep. Shall I walk you to your door?"

"Uh . . . no. No, thanks."

It was snowing harder now. Under a great weight of fatigue and grief, KaRawa plodded around the end of his dorm and in the front door. He could barely lift one foot after the other to climb the stairs. Once in his room he shut the door and fell onto his bed. And for an hour his body shook with great gasping sobs.

Waking at the breakfast bell, KaRawa found he was still sprawled on the bed in his parka and boots. For a moment he wondered why, and then he remembered the whole dreadful story. With a lump in his throat, he raced down the stairs and out into the morning. It was cold and dark, with heavy snow still falling. Apparently it had snowed all night, for the drifts were deep and the paths had not yet been cleared. He puffed his way to the healing house behind his dormitory and staggered in the door.

When he asked an assistant about Lani, she left and soon returned with Miwa.

"KaRawa, I think she had a good night," he reported. "She's breathing well and her color is a lot better than last night. She's still unconscious, however."

"What's wrong with her?"

The doctor drew a deep breath. He looked very tired.

"I want to be honest with you, son. It's serious. She has broken some bones in her back. I hope she will live, but I can't be sure."

KaRawa swallowed. "Can I . . . can I see her?"

"No, not yet. Maybe in a few days."

After breakfast, the entire training group went to the healing house together, where Miwa and Tiro spoke with them. Then Rok suggested that they take the morning off to rest from their grueling trip back from the Glacier.

It was not till after lunch on Fourth Day that they gathered again in the rescue hut to examine the maps they had made. All the maps were laid end to end on the floor, and Ukima walked along pointing out various features and the changes in the Glacier since the maps had been drawn the preceding spring. But when he came to the toe he paused.

"Who did this map?"

Holo answered, "KaRawa and I. Is there anything wrong?"

"Well, it's very nicely done. A beautiful map. But it looks as if you've made an error in your readings. You seem to show the toe of the Glacier about eighty paces farther down the valley than it should be. And where is the old trail hut? You don't show the hut below the Glacier at all."

"There was no hut," answered KaRawa.

"There what?" It was Rok, standing now and coming over to examine the map.

"We didn't see any hut. And we made our measurements very carefully," KaRawa replied. "Do you think the Glacier could have advanced that far since last year's maps were made?"

"Impossible!" snorted Rok.

But by the following evening the "impossible" was known throughout the village. Rok and another of the elders had left before dawn, hiked to the Glacier, checked out KaRawa and Holo's map, and returned. It was true. Since last spring the ice had advanced eighty to ninety paces down the valley. It had destroyed the hut, a trail, some huge fir trees along the side of the valley, and other landmarks.

The elders were calling a special evening meeting in the lodge. There was an uneasy tension in the air as people gathered. Word of Lani's injury and the Glacier's growth had everyone on edge. HaLona tried to bring the meeting to order, but nobody was listening to her.

"I told you the weather has been getting worse," shouted one of the old-timers. "The winters are longer and the summers are shorter. Just look at the snow out there today. It's supposed to be spring!"

"Yes, and that brute, the Glacier, grows more

powerful every year," cried another. "It killed the fur trader. It nearly killed the young woman day before yesterday. I say the day is coming when it will consume the village!"

"And that's not all!" An angry young man in the back was standing. It was Namok the blacksmith. "We have had more storms, more wild beasts, more bandits, more rescues to make, more deaths. That Glacier is evil. It's a sinister force controlling everything. It is out to destroy us all!"

"Nonsense!" another shouted. "It may be growing, but it's not a 'force' that makes things happen."

There were other agitated remarks, but finally HaLona was able to get everyone's attention. "Whether the Glacier is a living power in itself is a question we cannot answer. And in any case, there is nothing we can do about it. Our task . . . "

"There certainly is something we can do," Namok broke in again. "We can get out of here. With rescue work more hazardous every year, with this monster threatening our lives, I say it is time to give up and move below to safer ground."

There were several cries of "Yes! Yes!" but a loud chorus of "No!" drowned them out, and HaLona continued.

"Our task is to remain faithful as the Mountain Rescue Corps. The colder the winters, the more we shall be needed. Even if the entire year should turn to winter and the Glacier advance down to the plains, our mission is to rescue the lost. How else can we demonstrate the Southwind's care that we have known?"

"The Southwind, ha!" retorted the blacksmith. "If the Wind is so caring and so powerful, why doesn't it melt that Glacier right now!" And he stalked out of the meeting.

HaLona tried to calm everyone again, and then asked

for suggestions of how to deal with the advancing ice. A number of good ideas were given. Finally it was decided to set up a Glacier watch, a group of six persons to measure the ice's progress monthly and make recommendations to the council for action. The meeting ended with a song reaffirming the village's trust in the Wind, but KaRawa thought the singing was not so fervent as usual.

The unusually cold weather continued through the rest of the week, and it began to affect the attitude of villagers. People became more withdrawn, and tempers were short. Among the trainees, with the additional burden of Lani's injury on their minds, the mood was grim.

Morning, noon, and night, after every meal, KaRawa stopped by the healing house to ask if he could see Lani. Always the answer was "Not yet."

Finally, on First Day after supper, Miwa smiled and said, "Follow me."

The doctor led KaRawa down a short corridor to a door on the left, and opened it. From the doorway KaRawa could see a small, simple room with a bed, a table with a lamp burning, and over by the window a single chair. And there, in the bed, was Lani. Her braid had been undone, so that her long brown hair was all over the pillow. She seemed to be sleeping, breathing deeply, peacefully. But so far away.

"May I go in?"

"You certainly may. She is still unconscious but I'll leave you with her for a few minutes." And Miwa departed.

KaRawa took a few steps toward the bed.

"Lani?" He hadn't really planned what he would do when he saw her, but it seemed right to call her by name. "It's me. KaRawa."

No response.

He hesitated, then crossed the room and sat in the chair. Lani's face was silhouetted against the lamplight, and for a while he just watched her breathing. In and out. In and out. So regular. So quiet.

KaRawa's mind drifted back to the day of the accident. He could see again the ugly toe of the Glacier. He imagined for the thirtieth time the surface giving way under Lani and Ukima, and her tumbling headfirst into an icy pit. He began to feel a fire within, a growing rage.

"That Glacier!" he muttered aloud. His teeth were clenched and he stared fiercely at the opposite wall. "That monster! I hate it!"

All too soon Miwa was at the doorway signaling that it was time to go. With a last glance at Lani, KaRawa left the room, shuffled down the corridor, and stepped out into the snowy night.

Still angry and bewildered, he decided to give Akori a call. He found the caretaker sitting before the warm stove in his workroom.

"Come in, KaRawa," Akori called heartily. "I was just thinking that on a night like this an old man should have some young company."

The caretaker motioned to the empty chair beside him. KaRawa took a seat and soon felt the warmth of both the fire and the man.

"About the Glacier," he began. "Is it really an evil force, as some people say? I mean, does it control things?"

"So that's it. I thought you seemed to have a serious question on your mind. It's the Glacier, is it?"

"Yes. Does it make bad things happen?"

Akori gazed steadily into the coals of his little stove. When he spoke his voice was firm.

"In all the mountains there is only one supreme power—the power of the Southwind. In itself the

Glacier has no power to do evil, no power at all."

"But the Glacier is growing. You should see the toe. It's . . . "

Akori held up his hand. "KaRawa, there are many things that are not yet touched by the Southwind's power. You can appreciate that, for until recently you were among them."

"Yes."

"Some of these things are evil. Some of them are very strong, threatening our survival here, but the Southwind is stronger. The Southwind will overcome."

The Southwind will overcome. KaRawa wanted to believe this, but when he compared the soft spring breeze he had known in Fernvale with the awful advance of the Glacier, he had his doubts. Before he could voice his skepticism, Akori went on.

"I want to tell you something that not many people know. Are you listening?" Akori turned toward him, and KaRawa nodded.

"The Southwind has won! Although it may not seem so—with beasts and bandits, the cold, the Glacier—still the victory has already been assured. I give you my word. I guarantee it with my life: The loving power of the Wind has already won!"

For a while the only sound was an occasional sighing from the golden embers of the stove. KaRawa turned over in his mind what Akori had said. It was good news, good news indeed. Yet it was hard to accept. Finally he shared his misgivings.

"But the Wind is so small . . . just a breath on the cheek. And the Glacier is so immense, so cold, so relentless. I don't understand how the Wind . . . "

Akori smiled. "KaRawa, there's a story I haven't heard for a long time. Do you know it—the story of NaPiru and the acorn?"

KaRawa thought he had heard them all by now, but

he could not recall this one. The fire had died down somewhat, and the two pulled their chairs forward into the stove's warmth as Akori began.

Far, far off, in the ancient restless sea, there once was a large island called NaPiru, rugged and desolate. It was, in fact, a rocky desert, for no living thing grew there.

Now it chanced that the Southwind passed over NaPiru and took a liking to it. After all, the island did have a lovely shape, and the white crashing of the waves on its shore was a sight to behold. Thinking that the island would be much more beautiful if covered with growing things, the Wind considered how this might be done. But the sun was so hot that grass could not grow, and without any trees the birds could not build their nests. As the years passed and the Wind blew over land and sea, it lamented, "What can be done? How can I bring life to the island?"

A woodsman on the mainland, hearing the Wind's cry, called out. "O Wind of the South, I have here in my hand a forest, which you may plant on the island if you wish."

Hearing this, the Wind gusted down to have a look. "A forest indeed! How can you carry a forest in your hand?"

The woodsman opened his hand, and in his palm lay a fat, ripe acorn, brown and glossy in the sun.

"O Wind, many see the lowly acorn as merely the fruit of the oak tree, fit only for squirrels to eat. But as a woodsman I see in it the new oak that it will become, strong and gnarled with countless branches, the home of many small creatures. Further, I see all the acorns of that future oak, and all the oaks that they will become. I tell you, in my hand I hold a forest, and you are welcome to it."

Seeing that the woodsman spoke the truth, the Wind sent Ru the falcon to receive the acorn from the woodsman and carry it in his talons out to the island. There at the Wind's instruction, the bird dropped the acorn in a crack between two stones, and departed.

As the days passed the Wind cared for the acorn, sending warm rains across NaPiru, until at last the seed sprouted, and a small, green shoot climbed upward. Then the Wind took care that the sun shone a while each day, but also that clouds protected the seedling from too much heat.

Within a few years the shoot had grown into a strong sapling, and later a hardy young tree. By this time it was producing acorns of its own, which as the woodsman had foretold, grew into other saplings. The added shade allowed the small seeds that blew across the waters on the Wind to find cool, damp places to take root and grow. And the leafy branches provided nesting places for the birds from the mainland.

After many hundreds of years, the desert island became covered with a deep, green forest, and birdsong was heard from dawn to dusk. Now when the Southwind passes, it rustles through the trees and listens to the birds. And it is very pleased.

For a while KaRawa considered the story in silence. Then he said, "The acorn could have died, you know. Of all the acorns, not many actually become oak trees."

Akori chuckled and ran a hand through his thick gray hair. "Well, that's true. But the Southwind took care to see that the acorn lived, didn't it?"

"Yes," said KaRawa thoughtfully. "It did."

"KaRawa," said Akori after another pause, "you and I live in the day of the acorn. But I tell you, the Day of the Oak is coming! And there is no power that can stop its coming."

8

AT THE CHASM

The twelfth week of training had come, and it was time for another camp-out. Although it was cold and snow still lay deep on the ground, the trainees managed to hike down the South Track to Badger Flats and set up camp. But that night the temperature dropped further, and the next day they retreated to the village. By now all signs of spring had disappeared. The people of NaKoma shook their heads in disbelief: "Will it never end?"

KaRawa was glad to have the week in the village, for that gave him more time to be with Lani. Although he took part faithfully in the training program, he spent every free moment at the healing house in the chair by her window.

Lani's coma continued. Her eyes were closed, and she gave no sign that she heard or recognized him. But Miwa the doctor encouraged him to talk to her, and talk he did! On and on he went, sharing every detail of the training program, telling and retelling every story he had ever heard, inventing outlandish new stories that would normally have sent Lani into gales of laughter.

Still there was no response.

The following week the weather was no better. Although they could not work outdoors, the trainees met each morning in the rescue hut. They reviewed the maps they had already made. They practiced tying knots. They worked on techniques for restoring breathing and heartbeat. And of course, PaPaki kept them huffing and puffing with indoor exercises.

But KaRawa's mind was elsewhere. He could hardly wait till the afternoons, which were free, for then he could return to Lani's room. He was trying a new approach—telling a long, continuing story with many episodes, a story he called the Absolutely Amazing Adventures of Lani and KaRawa. He described how the lonely and fearful KaRawa was approached by Lani the wise, how she listened to him and encouraged him, how she foolishly let him risk his neck in the stone quarry—and then, after he'd nearly killed himself, introduced him to Akori the janitor.

"One sunny morning, a Seventh Day I believe it was, Lani the wise and KaRawa the fearful vowed to take a picnic lunch to Flat Top. Alas, it was almost a disaster! Lani the clumsy fell into the creek, causing KaRawa to spill the lunch, and one of the apples to roll into the water, never to be seen again." On and on he went.

Finally, on Fourth Night, he told Akori's tale of the island of NaPiru and the acorn. By then he was blinking back the tears.

"Oh, Lani! Don't you hear? Can't you see? The Day of the Oak is coming!"

He rushed out of the room, running smack into Rok. Glancing at KaRawa's red eyes, Rok extended a hand.

"Rough, eh? Has she improved any?"

KaRawa shook his head. Then he exploded: "Oh, Rok! I don't understand. Where's the Southwind when we need it? It's supposed to be so strong, so caring. It's supposed to be freeing and healing. With one little breath it could bring Lani back. What's going on? What is the Wind waiting for?"

Rok grasped the boy's shoulders. "Do you believe the Southwind has left you, KaRawa?"

"No . . . not really. In some ways it is stronger than ever. As I sit there with Lani, it seems to be softly blowing. I see it in the flame of the lamp. I feel it."

"Well then, do you think it has left Lani?"

"Yes, I'm afraid so." KaRawa hung his head. "If it were there it would heal her, wouldn't it?"

Rok took a deep breath. "KaRawa, did Lani ever speak to you of death?"

KaRawa thought a minute. "Yes, at the beginning— when I was so scared."

"Do you remember what she said?"

He struggled to recall. What was it? Ah . . . the words began to form in his mind. Slowly everything shifted. He could feel the tightness in his chest start to fade. He began to sense again some dependable center within, some promise that he had forgotten. He raised his eyes to Rok's.

"Yes. Yes, I remember. She said that her life rested on the Southwind and that she was ready to go wherever it blows. She said that she wasn't afraid of anything, that bad things would happen sometimes . . . even death. But it was all right because she was supported by the Wind, surrounded by it."

Rok nodded. "Do you agree?"

KaRawa glanced back through the doorway. Lani was still sleeping peacefully. Beside her on the table, the lamp flickered slightly. Then with a weak smile, he turned to Rok.

"Yes. Yes, it's all right."

Rok squeezed KaRawa's shoulders and looked deep into his eyes. Then the boy turned and left.

Just as KaRawa stepped out through the doorway of the healing house he heard the alarm sounding in the yard. The unseasonable weather of the last two weeks had caught many an unwary traveler in its clutches. The Mountain Rescue Corps had been busier than ever. KaRawa knew that rescuers assigned to duty tonight must be exhausted. Through a light snowfall he headed for the hut to watch the departure.

By now every detail of the rescuers' preparations had been memorized by KaRawa and practiced many times over in the course of training. Still he was fascinated by the activity in the hut. His mind wandered back to the night he had first met Lani here. How much he had changed since then! Yet he wondered, would he have the courage for a real rescue in the mountains on a night like this? To be honest, he didn't know for sure.

After the team disappeared up the trail, KaRawa returned to his room and went to bed. It seemed he had hardly fallen asleep when the bell rang a second time.

"Again?" he said aloud. He jumped to the window and looked out. "There aren't enough active rescuers for a second team. What'll they do?"

He struggled to dress, determined to keep his tradition of watching every departure. At the hut he found that Ukima was leading this team.

"Where to?" KaRawa asked.

"North. Somewhere this side of Elk Valley. It's rough up there, KaRawa."

"But the team—do you have enough?"

"Yes. We're only using six—four actives and two retired."

KaRawa watched in silence as the last of the dogs were leashed. When the team had left, KaRawa started back toward the dorm, but on the way he met Rok running toward him.

"KaRawa! I want you to prepare to go out as a rescuer if necessary."

"Me?"

"Yes. We're asking those of you in training and

several inactives to be on call in case of need. You probably won't be used, but get dressed for the mountains just in case."

His heart pounding, KaRawa hurried to his room and dressed for the trail—wool sweater, double wool pants, double wool socks, heavy boots. Then just as he was lacing his second boot, the alarm rang.

For a moment he froze. The great bell—it was calling *him!* He could feel the panic creeping over him, the old terror he thought he had conquered. *No! Not the mountains! Not on a night like this! Not the cold, dark unknown!* His stomach shriveled into a knot.

As a blind person may grope for a familiar wall or railing, KaRawa tried to reach out for support. What came to mind was Lani's confident words many weeks before: *KaRawa, you will do it!*

He finished dressing and stood in the dark room. *I will do it! Yes, I will do it!* But somehow, these were just words, empty words. Now, when he really needed the courage, it wasn't there. Trembling as much as ever, he slipped into his red parka and forced himself down the stairs and into the night.

At the hut Rok was in charge. He said that some travelers had been stranded by the storm somewhere beyond the Great Western Pass, that is, in unmapped territory not far from the Chasm. It was not clear just where they were, so three small teams of five persons each would head out together and then split to search different areas. There would be trainees and inactives in each group, and the leaders were to be Ilin, Rok, and Akori.

Akori! KaRawa was astonished. He had no idea that the caretaker would come out of retirement for such a mission. Then Rok announced that KaRawa would be on Akori's team, and his wonder turned to joy. There was no one he would rather follow on his very first rescue effort. Already he felt more confident.

He caught Akori's eye and smiled at him.

"I'm really glad to be on your team."

But Akori did not smile. "It's a dangerous mission, son. I don't know if we shall succeed."

"But the Wind . . . "

"The Wind will be with us, I know. But the Wind does not guarantee success."

It was chaos in the hut as fifteen persons scrambled to prepare at once. Equipment was in short supply, but the rescuers made the best of it. Finally they were ready, the lanterns were lit, and the party started up toward the pass. KaRawa was still shaking, but he didn't know if it was from fear, excitement, or the cold.

They marched along in silence, saving their energy for the urgent work ahead. Under Pine Bluff, past the cut-off to the Highland, up through the spruce grove. Up, up the switchbacks—the rescuers' pace was steady, strong, determined.

It was still snowing. As they approached the treeline, the gray light of day appeared and the lanterns were extinguished. In the cold, thin air their pace became slower, their breathing heavier. They passed the last of the dwarf fir trees clinging to life in the rocky heights. On and on. Around them was a shapeless, endless world of gray.

At last the trail began to level out, and KaRawa knew they had reached the Great Western Pass. The trail hut came into view through the swirling flakes, and they entered for a rest. For a time the rescuers just sat on the benches panting. Then Akori spoke.

"We need to be of one mind about continuing this mission."

Ilin shook his head. "It's almost hopeless to search for the stranded party in such a snowfall. There is danger that rescuers themselves could lose their way. I suggest we turn back."

Some nodded wearily in agreement.

"But there is the chance that the victims are still alive. Even nearby, eh?" Rok had thrown back his parka hood and was rubbing his head with a gloved hand. "We've come this far to find them, to save them. I believe we should continue the effort."

"Yes, that's what we're commissioned to do," added Ni.

Others expressed their views, and it was clear that most agreed with Rok. Finally it was decided to proceed.

While the other teams turned north and south, Akori led his group westward beyond the pass. He was followed by Hapu the beekeeper and Ni the tailor, both retired rescuers, then Simi and KaRawa from the training group. They stared through the snow and called and shouted, but found no one. Bearing somewhat to the north, they started along the lower slopes of the Bear—or at least KaRawa assumed that was where they were. The skies seemed to grow darker rather than lighter, and the snow flew so heavily that there was little chance of finding anyone. Every few paces they stopped to call out and listen, but there was no answer.

The farther they went, the thicker the snowflakes whirled around them. Soon KaRawa, who was bringing up the rear, could see only Ni and Simi in front of him, and then only Simi. Whenever they stopped to call, their cries were swallowed up by the driven snow. It was a world of gray and white, without a trace of life. KaRawa had never seen such a snowstorm.

Suddenly he thought he heard a sound off to his left, maybe a cry. He stopped to listen. Yes, he was sure! It sounded like a woman, or a child. Calling ahead to the others to follow him, he started down to the left. There it was again.

"Come on!" he shouted. But then with a jolt he realized that no one was answering and no one was following. He called again, but there was no reply. He was alone in the gray wilderness! He had violated the rule learned the first week of training: Never leave the rescue team.

He took a step upward, but then the muffled cry came again. Someone was near, just a few paces from where he stood. Cautiously he felt his way down the slope, peering in all directions. Ten steps, twenty, thirty. There was something ahead, something dark. Another step. It was bigger than a person, much bigger. Another step. It was . . .

"Yow!" With a cry KaRawa slipped and sprawled forward, down to the very edge of the darkness. Lying there, face down, he stared with horror into what seemed like a huge black hole. Even the swirling flakes were swallowed up in the darkness, lost in some infinite deep. It was, he knew at once, *the Chasm!*

In his terror he remembered the rescue team that had been swept into the Chasm by the avalanche, probably near this very spot. For one weird moment he found himself wondering if he could still see them falling, and strained to look.

"That's dumb," he mumbled aloud. "I've got to get out of here!"

There was nothing to hang on to. He tried to squirm his way backward up the slope, but this only dislodged the snow and ice under his chest. He watched as it fell out of sight into the darkness.

Gently he tried rolling to his left so that he could bend his head and shoulders around and upward, but he felt himself slipping in the snow. Suddenly he knew that he wasn't going to make it, that every movement was nudging his body farther over the edge. Already his chest was over. There was nothing he could do!

"KaRawa! Give me your hand!"

It was Akori's urgent voice behind him. KaRawa didn't have time to wonder how the caretaker had found him, for just then, with a *chunk!* another piece of the rim gave way beneath him.

"Akori . . . the edge . . . it's crumbling!"

"I know. Quick, your hand!"

"But it's dangerous. You'll . . . "

"Son, I know what I'm doing. Give me your left hand—*now!*"

Cautiously the boy stretched his arm backward along his body. He felt Akori's large hand grasp his wrist, then slowly pivot his upper body around and away from the precipice.

"Now listen to me, KaRawa. I have a good foothold here. Get hold of my body and pull yourself around so that you're on the uphill side of me. Then start up the slope—and I'll follow."

KaRawa turned his head enough to see Akori's face. His eyebrows were white with snow and his gray eyes flashed with a ferocity KaRawa had never seen.

"I . . . I don't think I can," he stammered weakly.

"Yes, you can! You can do it. And I'll be right with you."

KaRawa stretched his hand around Akori's left leg and tried to pull himself upward, but he didn't budge. Carefully turning he got a second hand around the leg and pulled with all his might. It worked. His chin was now even with Akori's boot. He hooked an elbow above the boot and pushed off. Then a knee, and he was safely above Akori. He rested a moment. Then he half crawled, half stepped—two, four, six, eight paces upward.

He was about to take another step when—*crack!*

There was a noise like thunder, a terrible splintering as if the mountain were exploding. Whipping around, KaRawa saw that just behind him the Chasm edge was giving way, and Akori with it!

"No!" KaRawa screamed. "No! No!"

There was no other sound. No cry from Akori. No noise of falling rock or ice. One moment the edge was there with the caretaker on it, and then it was not. There was—nothing.

KaRawa sank onto the snow. Akori was gone. Had it really happened? Yes, the caretaker had been there, and now he was gone! He could still picture Akori's face at that last instant. The caretaker's eyes were fixed on him, and they were—angry? No. Frightened? No. His eyes seemed to be shining with a glad determination and . . . love.

Slowly KaRawa shook his head. How could it be? How could anyone so full of light and life be gone? It was more than he could fathom. It was . . . too deep.

Then the dark truth struck him: "It's my fault," he mumbled to himself. "It's my fault. If I'd stayed with the others, it wouldn't have happened." He put his head down on his knees. "Akori died saving me from that Chasm, and it's my own fault."

For a long time the small figure sat hunched in the great gray expanse—limp, almost lifeless—too exhausted to move and too overcome even to cry.

Was it minutes, hours, days? His mind was numb. There was no time, no place.

Eventually he became aware of a change. He looked up. What was different? Why, the snow had stopped—stopped completely! It was still cloudy, but the storm was over. And there at his feet it lay—the Chasm. He could now see across to the other edge, maybe a hundred paces away. He could make out the sheer black wall dropping down, down, down.

KaRawa struggled to stand, for he wanted to do something, say something for Akori. What could it be? Tottering on weak legs, he thought a moment. Then, still facing the Chasm where the caretaker had fallen, he spoke aloud:

"Akori, I'm sorry. I'm sorry I left the team. I'm sorry you fell and . . . died." KaRawa swallowed, then continued.

"Thank you. Thank you, Akori, for rescuing me. For saving my life—when I was little. And now again."

A part of the song he had heard in his glen came to mind. And with a stronger voice, he sang now to his friend and teacher, his rescuer, Akori the caretaker:

O child of the Wind, the Wind, the Wind,
You are the one I love!

KaRawa hadn't expected a response—yet nonetheless it came. It was a sound—one long, low note, soft and sad, as if from a flute. No, several flutes. A sound of mourning. A slow, grieving music, far, far away. KaRawa strained to hear.

Little by little the sound brightened. Higher and faster it came, and louder—a music as if from hundreds of clear willow flutes on a spring morning. At first it was not really a song, just a beautiful chorus of sound. But then there seemed to be a melody. Yes, there was—a strange lilting tune, wonderfully joyful and free. It seemed familiar. Where had he heard it before? Then he remembered his first visit to Akori's workroom.

"It's Akori's song!" Still hardly believing, KaRawa whispered aloud. "Akori's song is coming from the Chasm! It's coming right up out of the Chasm!"

Now he felt a stirring of the thin mountain air. At first there was just a breath against his face. Then more. He lifted his chin and turned his head to the left in order to feel it. Yes, there was a little breeze flowing over him, gentle and warm.

"Warm? How can it be warm up here with nothing but snowy mountains?"

But warm it was, a mild and dancing breeze. Then he knew.

"It's the Southwind!" he cried. "And it . . . it's coming from the Chasm too. How can that be?"

In a moment KaRawa was wrapped in the Wind's soft embrace. He filled his lungs with the fresh, warm air and felt an astonishing new strength flood through his body. He took off his gloves—and for a time just bathed in the power of the Wind.

"It must be magic!" he cried. "Wait . . . it can't be. Akori said that there is no magic. It's just the Wind . . . the real and wonderful power of the Wind."

Although he could not explain it later, in that moment he knew beyond any doubt that Akori was not dead but was living in the Wind, that the care of Akori and the care of the Wind were the very same. And he now knew that he could give himself in trust to that care, that he could rest his whole life on it.

KaRawa's gaze followed the Chasm from left to right as far as he could see. It was still as black and ugly as before, but it had lost its grip on his spirit. There was no fear in him. No fear at all.

9

THE NEW STORY

Looking to his right, KaRawa followed the Chasm's winding course northward between mountain ranges—a dark rift in the pristine white of the snow. It was the same to the south. The abyss seemed to divide all the world in half. There on the Other Side were more mountains, more valleys, never explored by the Mountain Rescue Corps. And—who knows?—maybe other villages, other people.

KaRawa stepped forward to the very brink. The opposite wall plunged sharply down from the surrounding land—above was the white snow, then the sheer black wall of stone. His gaze followed the wall down, down. There was not a tree, not a shrub, not a sign of life all the way to the bottom.

"The bottom?" he gasped. "The bottom? This thing isn't supposed to *have* a bottom!" He had always heard that the Chasm dropped forever into an eternal night. Leaning forward, he looked more carefully.

"Why, it's a *canyon!*" he exclaimed. "It's the steepest and deepest I've ever seen. The sides go straight down to the bottom. But it *is* only canyon. There's a stream down there. Looks like a little gray thread from here."

KaRawa chuckled to himself. So this was the terrible Chasm! Somehow it had lost its dreadful mystery, its awful power. He now saw it and knew it for what it was—only a very deep canyon in the vast mountain landscape.

After one last look he turned from the Chasm and started up the slope. Now that the snowstorm was over, surely he could see if there were really any lost travelers in the area.

He had gone only a few paces when he spotted something blue in the snow off to his right. Rushing over and whisking away the snow, he was startled to find a parka—and then a face! It was a girl, maybe two or three years younger than he. Weakly she opened her eyes and tried to speak, but no sound came.

KaRawa shouted, "Can you hear me?"

The girl nodded.

"Do you think you are injured?"

She shook her head.

Furiously KaRawa dug away the snow and looked for any sign of blood. He cautiously moved her arms and legs, and noted that she did not wince. Then he spoke again, close to her ear.

"Is anyone else with you?"

Feebly she replied, "There were two. They fell."

"Fell? What do you mean, they fell? Where?"

"Into the gorge."

"You mean the black canyon? the Chasm?"

The girl nodded.

"Are you sure there is no one else?"

Closing her eyes, she shook her head. "No one."

KaRawa searched about for possible clues to others who might have been lost, but found nothing. Then back to the girl. Her face was as white as the snow, and he knew he had no time to lose.

"I'm going to lift you now, and carry you on my back. It won't be too comfortable, but it's the only way I can get you down where it's warm."

The girl did not respond. She seemed to have lost

consciousness. KaRawa took hold of an arm and a leg and carefully swung her body across his back. How light she seemed! How easily he strode up the slope! It was as if he were springing across the Highland on a summer afternoon. Where had this new strength come from?

Continuing upward, he came at last to a large snowy heap of rocks and circled around behind. Huddled in the sheltered spot were the other three members of the team.

When they saw him, they jumped up.

"Where have you been?" cried Ni. "Akori told us to wait here while he went to find you."

"Who's she? Is she hurt? Is she alive?" Simi was all questions.

"Where's Akori, anyway?" demanded Hapu.

There was no time for long explanations. Searching for some brief word, KaRawa replied simply, "Akori is in the Wind. He's in the Southwind."

The others looked at him in puzzled wonder. "He's what?"

But KaRawa decided that that was enough for now. He shifted the girl higher on his shoulders.

"Come on," he said with authority. "Follow me. We're heading back."

As the team returned along its earlier route below the Bear, the sky grew brighter and brighter. By the time they reached the Great Western Pass, the clouds had parted and the sun was shining. The sun! It seemed like months since they had seen it. The gray and white wilderness all around them was transformed into dazzling silver.

At the trail hut they paused for a quick lunch of bread and cheese. Although they tried to offer some to the girl, she slept on. Then Hapu hoisted her to his shoulders, and they started down the trail.

Later, below treeline, they stopped to make a litter out of branches and rope. The sun's warmth seemed to be having its effect on the girl, for she opened her eyes as they transferred her to the litter. Overhead in the blue, a falcon was soaring on its long, pointed wings. The girl followed it with her gaze, and smiled.

By late afternoon KaRawa's team could see the rescue hut. Apparently his was the last group to return, for the place was swarming with rescuers. When they saw the team with the litter approaching, a great cheer went up, and several ran out to meet them.

"Are you all right?" shouted Rok.

"Why, it's a girl! Is she injured?"

"Where's Akori? Is he behind you?"

It seemed that everyone had a question. KaRawa's own questions were quickly answered. All the other rescue efforts of the night before had been successful, and everyone had returned safely.

Rok was beaming. "That's quite a record for a bunch of inactives and trainees, eh?"

Someone asked if the girl had been traveling alone. KaRawa explained that her two companions had apparently fallen into the Chasm.

"Did you really see the Chasm?" another asked.

"Where's Akori?"

"Wait!" said Rok. "We're all exhausted. Let's go into the hut where we can sit down. Then KaRawa can tell us about it."

Tiro and some others hustled the girl to the healing house while everyone else crowded into the hut and found seats, some on benches, some on the floor. KaRawa sat on the edge of a table. There seemed to be only one way to say it.

"Akori . . . Akori fell into the Chasm."

"Oh, no!"

"Not Akori! Not in the Chasm!"

"It can't be! Are you sure?"

KaRawa nodded his head, and soon all was quiet. Some rescuers put their hands to their faces. Others slumped and dropped their gaze to the floor, or reached to their neighbors for comfort.

"It was all my fault," KaRawa continued. "I became separated from the team when I heard the girl calling. In trying to find her, I slipped."

He went on to describe his ordeal at the brink of the Chasm, Akori's help, and then the terrible splintering of the edge and Akori's fall.

In the rescue hut there was not a sound. All seemed overcome by the news. The very thought of the Chasm was bad enough, but to learn that the beloved caretaker had met his death there—that was almost more than the rescuers could bear.

"But that wasn't the end," KaRawa continued. "I can't explain what happened next. There was something like music, like flutes, hundreds of flutes. And it turned into a gentle breeze, soft and warm. I couldn't believe it. A spring breeze was coming right out of the Chasm."

KaRawa was standing now, gesturing with out-stretched arms.

"It just encircled me with . . . well, with care and power. It was the Southwind, you see! And somehow Akori was in the Wind. Akori was alive in the Wind, caring for me!"

By now all faces were turned toward KaRawa. Some people were open-mouthed with surprise. Others were frowning skeptically.

"Then I went over to the Chasm," said KaRawa. "I stood there and looked right down into it. And I felt that somehow I had conquered it—that Akori and the Southwind and I had beaten that old Chasm, and it was just a deep, ugly hole in the ground."

Some of the rescuers exchanged questioning glances.

"And I noticed something strange. I'd always heard that

the Chasm was bottomless, that it dropped forever into the black. But it isn't like that. I could see the bottom! It's only a canyon, a really deep canyon. I saw a stream down there."

"A canyon? Are you sure?" Ukima seemed doubtful.

"I'm sure. If we had ever mapped beyond the Great Western Pass we would have discovered this long ago."

"I guess," began Ilin reflectively, "I guess we were too frightened to try. We never dared to go near the thing."

Rok rose and came across the hut to KaRawa, extending his hands. For a moment he held KaRawa's hands in his, looking into his eyes. Then he turned to the group.

"As far as I know, no one of our village or any village has ever willingly stood at the very edge of the Chasm . . . willingly peered into its depths. Until now it has been too terrible, too black and mysterious. I don't understand what has happened with Akori's death. I don't understand what KaRawa means, that Akori is alive in the Wind. But I do know that something has changed."

There were quiet murmurs of agreement.

"At least it has changed for KaRawa." He turned to the boy. "I know that Akori's death is a great loss to you, KaRawa. It is a loss to our whole village. He was one of our greatest rescuers—faithful, wise, strong. He can never be replaced. I only hope that what you say will prove to be true—that he is, in a sense, still our caretaker in the blowing of the Southwind."

"I believe he is," replied KaRawa firmly. But he was swaying on his feet as he spoke. Rok seemed to sense his fatigue.

"It's been a long night, a long day. I suggest we all get some rest, eh?"

As they left the hut, several of the rescuers gave KaRawa a friendly clap on the shoulders, but they were all too weary for more talk.

Of course KaRawa made a stop at the healing house before going to his dorm. As he opened Lani's door he half expected to find a change in her as well. But she was the same, still sleeping the deepest of sleeps.

He stayed only a moment, just long enough to whisper at her ear: "Lani, good news! It's really true—the Southwind has *won!*"

On Seventh Night a special meeting was held in the lodge to remember Akori the caretaker and celebrate his life. After beginning with songs, people around the circle, one by one, stood and told of their experiences with Akori. A child described how the janitor had helped a cut finger to heal. A teenager shared some wise counsel Akori had offered during a time of conflict. An older woman told how one of his stories had helped her to sense the Wind blowing in her life.

KaRawa was most surprised to learn that so many of the people of NaKoma had been saved by Akori during his younger days as an active rescuer. There must have been a dozen or more who owed their lives to him. Truly, the caretaker had been very important to many villagers. He was deeply loved by all.

Later KaRawa was asked to share his experience at the Chasm. He retold the story, trying to remember every detail. As he spoke to the village family around the circle, the tale seemed to take on even more importance. He became aware that this was a brand new story, now to be added to the vast fund of stories shared by the village. He could almost hear trainees of future generations say, "Tell us the one about Akori at the Chasm."

"You know," he continued, "last week I shared the tale Akori told me, the story of the island NaPiru, the woodsman, the Wind, and the acorn."

Several heads nodded.

"Friends, I think Akori was our woodsman. He was
telling us a story about himself. He was the one who
could see the forest in the acorn. He was the one who
best understood the power of the Wind's care."

He looked around the circle. Every eye was on him.

"You see, Akori told me that the Southwind has
already won. He said that we're living now in the day of
the acorn, but the Day of the Oak is coming!"

KaRawa paused briefly. "I don't know exactly what
that means. When I first heard it, I wasn't sure I
believed it. But since standing at the edge of the Chasm,
with the Southwind in my face, I know it's true."

After KaRawa sat down, the leader announced the
closing song, and the lyre chords filled the lodge. With
steady assurance the people of NaKoma sang together.

The beginnings we make, so helpless and small,
Are beginnings we make in you.
From the day of our birth we follow the call,
We travel with you, we do!
   So breathe on us, breathe on us, traveling Wind.
   Breathe on us all as we go.

The journeys we take, whether easy or steep,
Are journeys we take in you.
Onto the high road from out of the deep,
We travel with you, we do!
   So breathe on us, breathe on us, traveling Wind,
   Breathe on us all as we go.

The endings we find, whether early or late,
Are endings we find in you.
And there in the sunlight we know you await,
We travel with you, we do!
   So breathe on us, breathe on us, traveling Wind,
   Breathe on us all as we go.

10

TWO BROWN ACORNS

Day after day the warm sun shone, melting away the great drifts of snow. Puddles and streamlets formed all over the village, and below in the ravine, Cub Creek became a raging torrent. It was spring at last!

The stunted leaves resumed their interrupted growth —maple, birch, hickory, and oak, in twenty delicate shades of green. In the grove on the way to the stone quarry, there was now no mistaking the fresh green needles at the end of every hemlock branch. Chipmunks came out of hiding. On the hillsides, mother bears were seen foraging with their cubs. From morning till night, the forest echoed with the clear liquid song of the wood thrush, while deep in the shade of KaRawa's glen, in the rich black earth, the maple seeds were taking root.

The last week of the training program had come— and finally, the morning of Sixth Day, the very last session. This would have been a day of rollicking celebration, except for Lani's condition. Ever since her injury the group had been subdued. Today was no different.

Rok had previously announced that the only work trainees would do today would be to share their answers to the question he had posed weeks before:

Why do you intend to be a mountain rescuer? In order
to be commissioned, each person would need to
answer this question.

So today the trainees sat quietly in the rescue hut,
and Rok called on them one by one, beginning with
Simi, the oldest.

"Well," she answered, "I believe that the important
thing is always human life. If there is any possibility
that a life can be saved, we have to try. After all, we are
all brothers and sisters in one big human family." She
went on to share her dedication to being a lifesaver.

WaLoka was next. He emphasized his deep desire to
be a useful member of the village family. Kato, who had
once been rescued herself said it was only right that she
should rescue others. And so on, one after another.

"Okay, KaRawa, how about you?"

There had been a time when the question of *why*
made KaRawa uneasy. His reasons had been a riddle,
even to himself. As he had told Lani weeks before,
becoming a rescuer was just something he felt he had to
do. It was in his bones.

But a lot had happened to him in the past few
months. It was almost as if he were a new person. So as
he started to answer, his mind was clear, his voice full
and sure.

"I want to become a mountain rescuer so that I can
show with my life how the Southwind cares for
everyone. Since we started training, I've really come to
sense the blowing of the Wind. As you remember, I've
learned that no matter how much or little I achieve, no
matter how good or bad I act, the Wind is there holding
me, surrounding me, breathing its life into me . . . and
the same is true for everybody."

KaRawa paused to look around the circle.

"Well, I want the Wind to blow through me for

others, just as it has for me through Akori and Lani and all of you. I want a part in sharing the Wind's care. For me, the best way to do this is to try to help those who are most lonely, most hurt, most desperate—the lost of the mountains.

He looked at Rok. "I guess that's it."

"Well said, KaRawa!" Rok responded. "Each of you has shown a good understanding of the reasons for rescue work and a full commitment to the task." With a twinkle in his eye, he continued:

"So it is now my privilege to announce that you young men and women have completed the requirements for preparation as mountain rescuers. Your trainers are recommending you all to the elders for commissioning!"

"Yowee!"

"Rescuers! Rescuers! We're rescuers!"

Suddenly everyone was laughing and hugging and slapping one another on the back, trainees and leaders alike. What a tumult! It was as if all the tension of fifteen weeks of running and mapping and studying, even of injury and death, were released at once.

"Excuse me! May I have your attention? Excuse me, everyone!" It was Tiro's voice cutting through the din. Finally she stood on a bench, and the group calmed down enough to hear.

"Sorry to interrupt your celebration, but I thought you should know. I've just come from the healing house. Lani asked me to say hello to everyone."

There was a long second of absolute silence. Then KaRawa's voice:

"Lani? Lani said what?"

Tiro was beaming. "Lani asked me to greet you and give you her love."

Before Tiro's words were out, the shouting began

again—a laughing and crying and jumping all at once, a
wild dancing for joy.

"Lani!" was all that anyone could say. "Lani! Lani!
Lani!" The hut had never witnessed such a ringing
jubilee.

Under PaPaki's training program, KaRawa had
become one of the fastest runners of the village. But
never before had he run as he did now—reaching the
healing house, it seemed, in a single breath. Miwa was
standing by the entrance and tried to speak to him, but
KaRawa sped right past, down the corridor, and to
Lani's door.

He stopped short, panting, then quietly opened the
door. The patient lay still in bed, her face turned away
toward the window—and for a moment everything
looked the same. But then Lani slowly turned her head,
and her eyes found him in the doorway.

"Well, rescuer," she asked weakly, "where have you
been?"

Her voice seemed distant and strange, but KaRawa
could see that her eyes were full of the old mischief.
Smiling, he walked slowly around the bed and sat in the
chair by the window, where he had spent so many
hours over the past weeks.

With a casual air, he replied, "Oh, I've just been
fooling around out in the quarry. Trying to learn to
climb, you know."

"Still?" she asked. "You sure must be a slow
learner!"

"Well, I've improved a lot in climbing up, but I'm still
sort of awkward at falling down."

"Really? I always thought falling down was one of
your best talents!"

He laughed, but then leaned forward.

"Lani, I . . . I'm so glad you're better. I was really

scared. I didn't know what was happening. I thought you might . . . you know . . . die or something."

"They say I've been here four weeks. I can't believe it. It seems as if we just went out to map the Glacier yesterday."

"To me it seems as if you've been here four months. It's been . . . forever!"

With one hand Lani brushed her hair back, and smiled. "Tiro says you came every day, several times a day. Did you really?"

"Yes. I told you stories."

"Thanks, KaRawa. Thanks for . . . caring. I'm afraid I didn't hear the stories though. The first thing I heard was the singing of the birds this morning. It must really be spring."

"It sure is!" replied KaRawa. "It's beautiful out there. We need to get up to the Highland. They say the bell-flowers are blooming. When can you go?"

Lani's gaze fell. She started examining the edge of her blanket.

"Well, maybe you should go with Holo or someone."

"Oh, no. It can wait. How about next week?"

Lani's large brown eyes searched KaRawa's. "They haven't told you, have they?"

"Told me? Told me what?"

"KaRawa . . . I can't . . . I can't walk. My legs just don't work. The doctor says I'll never be able to walk."

KaRawa bit his lip and sputtered. "No! They don't know . . . I mean . . . well . . . it *can't* be!"

"It's true. There are some broken bones in my back. I seem to be paralyzed from the waist on down. That's the way it is."

KaRawa saw that Miwa was now standing in the doorway. The doctor nodded gravely. KaRawa swallowed and looked at the floor.

"It's all right," continued Lani. "This morning, ever

since they told me, I've been thinking about it. It's really not so bad. I mean, there are lots of things I can do without walking." She paused. "Well . . . I can . . . " but her voice broke. And drawing her hands over her face, she started to shake.

KaRawa looked up at Miwa, not certain how to respond to Lani's tears. The doctor came over to Lani's bed and gently rested a hand on her quavering shoulder. KaRawa rose to go, but Miwa shook his head. So KaRawa took a seat at the foot of the bed—and for a long time the silent tears flowed.

Sitting there, he noticed the curtain moving slightly in the spring breeze. Smiling, he nodded to himself. *The Southwind has many ways.*

Finally she was asleep, and KaRawa and Miwa tiptoed out.

On Seventh Day, KaRawa woke with a clear sense of what he must do. Before breakfast, he stopped by for a quick visit with Lani. Then after the meal he spoke to Holo.

"Are you busy today?"

"Not really. Do you want to do something?"

"Yes, there's a place I want to show you. How about taking a lunch?"

"Sounds great!" Holo answered, and the two went to the kitchen where they packed bread, cheese, boiled eggs, and raisins. In a few minutes they were leaving the village and heading down the ravine. In places, Cub Creek was so high that it flooded the trail, and its usual merry babble was more like a roar.

"What a day!" shouted KaRawa.

"You said it!" Holo replied. "Just look at that sky!"

It was one of those rare spring mornings when the air

is perfect—warm in the sunshine but refreshingly cool in the shadows, with just a hint of a breeze caressing the skin. Up beyond the birches' white trunks and trembling green leaves the sky was its deepest blue, and seemed close enough to touch.

At the three boulders KaRawa stopped. "Have you ever been up here?"

"No, what is it?"

"Well, if you're running a race it's a shortcut . . . "

"Oh-ho, now I get it!"

"But it's more than that to me. Come on."

KaRawa led Holo between the stones and up into the glen beyond. The sun was shining through the half-grown leaves with shifting patterns of light and shade. Here and then the deep purple of violets caught the eye, or a gleaming diamond of dew on the moss. And all across the little valley, new green ferns—thousands of ferns—were opening their coiled fronds to the light.

KaRawa and Holo were spellbound by the beauty of the place. It was not until they came to his stone that KaRawa spoke:

"This is my private place. I call it Fernvale."

"It's beautiful! I didn't know it was here."

"As far as I know, nobody else does. I haven't shown it to anyone before . . . not even to Lani."

Holo glanced at him quizzically.

"Somehow I wanted you to see it," KaRawa added.

Holo stammered. "I . . . I don't know what to say. I'm glad to be here."

The two spent the morning exploring the glen. They clambered over the rocks around the rim. They climbed a couple of the larger maple trees and then started to count the many ferns—but gave up after four hundred. After a while they returned to KaRawa's rock and sat down for a rest. The talk turned to Lani. "Holo," said KaRawa, "I want you to help me do something."

"What is it?"

"Someday I want you and me to help Lani walk down here. I want to show her Fernvale."

Holo looked doubtful. "Well . . . yes. But they say she's never going to walk again. I don't think it's too smart to plan for something that's impossible. Maybe we could get a litter and . . . "

"No, I said *walk*. And it's not impossible. I think . . . I think that with the Southwind nothing is impossible."

"Well . . . "

"I didn't say next week, or next month, or even next year. I said *someday*. Holo, will you help me? With the Wind we can do it!"

With wondering eyes Holo returned KaRawa's gaze. Then he smiled broadly.

"Yes! I'll help you. We can do it!"

"We *will* do it!" confirmed KaRawa.

After eating their lunch the boys left the glen and ambled slowly up the trail. At the village they decided to call on Lani, and found her in a jolly mood. They talked of training adventures, of the instructors they had come to admire so much, of spring and sunshine and birdsong. On and on they went.

At last the supper bell rang, and the boys left. On their way to the hall, they were joined by Tiro.

"You know, KaRawa, there's someone else at the healing house who could use a visit."

"What? Who do you mean?"

"The girl you rescued at the Chasm."

"Oh, I forgot all about her. How is she doing?"

"She had some frostbite, but she'll be fine. She wants to meet her rescuer."

"Fine!" said KaRawa. "I'll be there after supper."

But at supper he learned that the instructors had planned a special party for the trainees that evening. By the time the party was over, it was late, so postponing his visit to another time, KaRawa went to bed.

He woke early the next morning, refreshed and excited. It was First Day. The Commissioning of Rescuers would be held in just a few hours as part of the regular First Day meeting of the village. At last!

He sat at his window watching the yard below brighten in the morning light. How long before, it now seemed—that night he had watched from here just after the alarm sounded, the night this whole, strange journey had begun!

At breakfast he exchanged excited nonsense with other trainees.

"Bad news! I hear PaPaki is going to make you run to the Bear and back before you're commissioned!"

"Well, I hear you were flunked for forgetting to map Rok's bald spot!"

Before going to the lodge, KaRawa stopped briefly at Lani's room in the healing house. As he entered, her face lit up.

"Well, if it isn't the mountain rescuer. Congratulations!"

KaRawa smiled a small, embarrassed smile. "Thank you."

"What did I tell you months ago? I said, 'KaRawa, you will do it!' Didn't I say that? Well, here you are—and you have done it!"

"I must admit that you were right, as usual. But I just wish you were being commissioned too."

Lani's smile faded. "So do I. You know, I had begun

to think that I might make a good rescuer—and now it hurts never to be one."

KaRawa put his hand on her bed. "Lani, don't say *never.*"

Her eyes questioned his.

"*Never* is another of those words like *silly,*" he continued. "With the Southwind around, it's just better not to use words like that."

"All right," she smiled. "If you say so."

"I say so."

"You know, I was thinking last night. Maybe there's something good that can come out of this . . . this condition of mine. It could be very hard on my wolf."

"Your pride? How's that?"

"Well, it could teach me something. I might learn to be a more open person. You know . . . more ready to depend on others, learn from others. More modest."

KaRawa grinned. "More modest? Don't count on it!"

"Get out of here!" Lani laughed. "You'll be late for the meeting."

With a wave KaRawa turned and went straight to the lodge. There, as people gathered around the fire, the big news was Lani's improved condition. During the opening of the meeting, KaRawa was the first to express his joy and thanks, and many others followed.

Next, as usual, came the singing. By now all the songs were familiar to KaRawa, and several had very special meaning. He was especially pleased to join in singing the song he had heard at Fernvale: "O child of the Wind." At a previous meeting he and Lis had taught this new song to the villagers, and by now it was a favorite of all.

Then HaLona told the story of a mountain rescue some years before KaRawa had come to the village. To KaRawa it was a new tale. How surprised he was to learn that the hero, the leader of the rescue party, had been Akori! KaRawa felt all warm inside. It was good to have Akori take part in his commissioning day through this story.

During the customary time of silence that followed, feelings of many kinds filled KaRawa's heart. He was glad for his new friends and proud of their achievements as a training group. He was awed by the challenge that lay ahead, saving lives in the mountains. Most of all, he was thankful for the touch of the Southwind in his life.

The Commissioning of Rescuers was held during the decision time at the end of the meeting. HaLona called out the seven names—"Simi . . . WaLoka . . . Kato . . . Lis . . . Holo . . . PaWito . . . KaRawa." One by one they came forward and faced the family with their backs to the Ever Flame. Rok then stood by them and spoke to the villagers, saying a few words about each trainee—his or her strengths and an amusing episode or two. It was all lighthearted, and the entire village joined in laughter.

Then old Ta rose and came forward. He asked the trainees to turn and face the fire as they took the Rescuers' Vows:

"Do you promise to be open to the Southwind, to trust your whole self to its power and care, and to follow wherever it blows?"

The trainees answered, "We do!"

"Do you promise to keep yourself in readiness for the demanding work of mountain rescues, to maintain an alert mind and a fit body so that you may be equal to whatever challenge may come?"

"We do!"

"Do you promise that, whenever you are on duty, you will answer the alarm when it sounds and devote your every effort to rescuing the lost, the stranded, and the injured?"

"We do!"

Rok and Ta then came to each trainee, one taking one hand and one the other. With words as old as the village itself, each in turn was commissioned as a mountain rescuer.

As the youngest, KaRawa was still last, so that he was more than ready when his turn came. The two grasped his hands firmly and looked him straight in the eye:

"KaRawa, with breath given us by the Wind, we commission you as a rescuer of NaKoma, the Mountain Rescue Corps."

KaRawa thought that the commissioning was now complete, but Rok had a surprise.

"Finally, I want to give each of these seven rescuers a little token to remember our training by. Each object is different, a symbol of some important part of the weeks we spent together."

Again Rok came down the line, speaking softly to each. When he came to KaRawa, Rok said simply, "These are for you and Lani. You'll know what they mean."

Looking down into his hands, KaRawa saw two acorns, plump and brown and glossy.

And in a gentle gust of the Southwind, the Ever Flame danced.